Thalia De Luca

JACLIN MARIE

Copyright © 2022 Jaclin Marie
All rights reserved

The characters and events portrayed in this book are fictitious. Any similarity to real persons, living or dead, is coincidental and not intended by the author.

No part of this book may be reproduced, or stored in a retrieval system, or transmitted in any form or by any means, electronic, mechanical, photocopying, recording, or otherwise, without express written permission of the publisher.

ISBN- 9798449155221

Cover by: Acacia Heather
Editing by: Antonia Salazar
Library of Congress Control Number: 2018675309
Printed in the United States of America

To all the good girls who turned bad.

Playlist

"Baby you want it, yeah
Slow it down if you need to
Show me how just to please you
Work it out in the sheets
Do me and see through
I want you feel you"
Shut Up and Listen
- Nicholas Bonnin & Angelicca

I Was Never There **THE WEEKND**
Bound 2 **KANYE**
Hymn for the Weekend **COLDPLAY**
Fuck Love **TRIPPIE REDD**
Undercover **SELENA GOMEZ**
Sex With Me **RIHANNA**
Earned It **THE WEEKEND**

Die For You **THE WEEKEND**
Feel A Way **H.E.R.**
Habits Of My Heart **JAYMES YOUNG**
This Could Be Us **RAE SREMMURD**
Don't Wanna Fall In Love **KYLE**
Close **NICK JONAS**
Hands To Myself **SELENA GOMEZ**
Dangerous Woman **ARIANA GRANDE**
Be Together **MAJOR LAZER**
Often **THE WEEKND**
I Wanna Be Yours **ARCTIC MONKEYS**
Dirty **TANK**
Acquainted **THE WEEKEND**
Love Me Now **JOHN LEGEND**
Selfish Love **DJ SNAKE**
Fall In Love **$NOT**
Young Dumb & Broke **KHALID**
Heartless **MADISON BEER**
Smells Like Teen Spirit **NIRVANA**

Prologue

FIFTEEN YEARS AGO

"Surprise!" my parents and Alexander's say as they smile at us with open arms.

A smile falls on my lips as I take in what's behind them and around Alexander and me.

A farm.

Mommy and daddy got me a farm.

I run to mommy and wrap my arms around her. "Thank you, thank you, thank you. I love it so much." Mommy hugs me back and I can feel her smile as she puts her cheek against mine.

I let go of her and go to hug daddy. "I hope you like it, *la mia principessa*," he whispers in my ear before kissing my forehead.

I let go of him and smile so hard my teeth almost fall out. "I love it so much. Alexander and I are going to have so much fun," I say before looking at Alexander who has a small smile that threatens to fall on his lips.

I know he is happy.

He is just a boy and boys don't like to smile.

I asked mommy one time why boys don't like smiling and she just told me that boys are stupid.

Alexander isn't stupid though.

He's so smart and cool.

I wish I could be as cool as him.

Alexander is my best friend, other than Jane but she doesn't even talk that much yet but I know we will be best friends too.

"Alexander! Let's go play!" I say as I run towards him and wrap my arms around his stomach.

"Yeah, kids. Go play. Check out all of the animals," Emma, Alexander's mom says as she smiles down at us.

I let go of Alexander and jump up and down before running towards where the horses are.

Horses are my favorite animal.

They are so pretty.

"What's your favorite animal, Alexander?" I look at him and he looks away from the horses to look down at me.

At six years old, Alexander is tall.

He is almost as tall as the big kids in our school.

But it's a good thing he is tall because then he can beat people up who are mean to me.

Last week Kevin, a mean kid who is in Alexander's grade, pushed me off the swing. Before I could even say something to him and push him back, Alexander pushed him to the ground and slapped him on the face.

I like seeing him fight. I smiled when I saw Alexander do that for me.

That's why he is my favorite person in the world. I love mommy and daddy, but I also love Alexander.

Sometimes he is mean, but he always says sorry when he is mean.

"I like whatever you like," he says and I feel myself smile again.

"Let's ride one of the horses, Alexander!" I say before running towards the stables.

Alexander follows me, running almost as fast as me. I laugh as we race to see who can get to the stables first.

"Beat ya!" Alexander yells once he touches the stables that hold a horse.

I rest my hands on my knees, trying to catch my breath. "Not . . . fair." Alexander breathes in and out as he smiles at me. By the time we are done catching our breaths, we both start walking down to the barn to look at the horses. I see a pretty black one which makes me smile again and walk closer to it. "Look at this one, Alexander. He is so pretty." I look at Alexander and see him looking at me with a smile on his face.

I smile back at him and look up at the horse. I reach out to touch his head that is hanging out of the stable but instead I touch his nose, a hand grabs mine and turns me around to make me face a man with a dark skin tone and white hair on his face.

"Don't be touching things that will hurt you, little bit," he says and I feel my heart race as I try to get my hand out of his grip.

"Hey, let go of her," Alexander says as he grabs my hand and takes my wrist out of the man's hold.

The man stands straight, and he looks like a giant as he towers over us.

The man was about to say something but then I hear daddy

yell my name making me turn my head and see him at the entrance of the stables.

"Daddy!" I yell as I run towards him. "He tried to take me away. Say '*saluta da parte mia satana*' to him and make him light up!"

Daddy starts laughing and shakes his head as he kneels, so he is the same height as me. "Baby, he isn't trying to hurt you. He is just making sure you won't get hurt with the horses. They can be dangerous *la mia principessa*," daddy says as he moves the hair out of my face. He then looks up at the man behind us. "Did something happen?"

"Thalia tried to touch Nyx. He is the new horse I told you about. The one that has issues."

My dad nods his head and looks back at me. "The horse you were about to touch is dangerous. It's good you didn't touch him."

"But I want to ride one."

"Okay. You can ride one. Just one that fits your size, Thalia," daddy stands up and grabs my hand and Alexander's, who is next to me. "Let's go find a good horse for you guys to ride and then you can explore the rest of the land, okay?"

Alexander ended up getting a white horse and I asked daddy if I could get a black one so he gave me a black one.

I wanted to ride the bigger black ones, but daddy said it was too dangerous.

As Alexander and I ride the horse, mommy holds my hand while taking pictures. Daddy and Alexander's dad, Leo, are walking behind us while Emma and mommy are next to us. I wanted mommy to ride with me, but daddy said she couldn't because she was holding my baby brother in her stomach.

Alexander wants to go faster on the horse but the guy from the stables, whose name is Luca, told him to not go fast since this was his first time riding the horse.

After Alexander and I are done riding the horses, mommy and daddy tell us to go look around the farm some more.

When Alexander and I walk past the chicken pen, I start walking a little faster than him because I hate chickens. He laughs but doesn't tease me. Instead, he makes us go the opposite way so I won't be scared.

That's one of the things I love most about him, he always looks out for me and makes sure I am okay.

Now, Alexander and I are sitting on the grass where there are small flowers around us.

"What do you want to do when you are bigger? Like as an adult like our moms and dads?" I ask Alexander and he looks at me as he picks the grass.

He shrugs his shoulders, "I don't know. I kind of like what they do."

"How they make people turn red?" Alexander laughs and nods his head. "It's so weird that we are getting older. You're already six!"

"I'm happy we share a birthday," Alexander says and I see him pick a flower from the grass. He turns his head to look at me and he extends his hand to mine and offers me the flower. "Happy birthday Thalia. I love you."

I smile and my face feels like it's on fire. "Thank you, thank you, thank you," I take the flower from him and wrap my arms around his head to hug him. "I love you too, Alexander."

Alexander and I hug for what feels like forever but then I hear daddy calling my name making me release Alexander and stand up. I see daddy who is waving at me from down the small hill that Alexander and I are sitting on.

I look at Alexander. "I have to go. Are you coming?"

"I will go in a little bit," Alexander says and he smiles at me.

"Okay. I'll see you later," I give him one last smile before running down the hill.

I look at the flower Alexander gave me and look back down at my dad as I put the flower in my back pocket.

I'll keep it forever.

One

SIX YEARS AGO

"God, he is hot. I wish he could take my virginity," Becca says as she rolls her eyes to the back of her head.

I almost gag just from hearing her talk about him.

"No, same. I once heard that he beat up one of the senior Calcio players. No one goes after those dudes," Regina agrees and I can almost hear her moan from just sitting next to her.

"You guys are both disgusting for wanting someone like him. Trust me he isn't all that."

Regina looks away from him and looks at me with a raised eyebrow, "Aren't you guys like cousins?"

I cringe when she says that. "No, we're not fucking cousins you dumbass. His father is my father's best friend."

"Lucky. So, you get to fuck him."

I can't help but laugh.

Yea.

Like Alexander and I will ever be fucking one another.

"Why would you even suggest that? That's stupid, I have no clue where you get these ideas, Regina. I will never be fucking Alexander. I have better things to do than obsess over him like you and the rest of these stupid little girls at this school do. I'm better than that."

"You guys would kind of look good together not going to lie," Becca says and I just roll my eyes at her for the fifth time today.

I look away from the food on my plate and look at Alexander who is sitting at the opposite table across the room. I feel my body fill with heat. My hands clench by my side and I can't help but feel my heart rate speed up.

Fuck you, Xander Russo.

Alexander smirks at me and then winks.

I bite the inside of my cheek and try to ignore the churn in my stomach.

God, I feel like I'm going to throw up.

Alexander Russo.

So many ways to describe the type of person he is.

He is worse than the nightmares under my bed. He isn't a good guy like the other guys at this school.

No.

Alexander Russo is a jackass and if my dad wasn't named the number one devil in the world, Alexander would take that spot.

He is only sixteen, but he has done so much damage that it would probably scare all of these little girls away.

I've seen everything he has done.

Sometimes I find myself wanting to be that deranged in the way he is.

My father and his father are business partners but not in the way you think. Everyone at this school thinks my dad is just some rich CEO who owns billion dollar companies but it's actually the complete opposite. Now don't get me wrong, he does own companies but not the kind you think.

Alexander's father is second in command for my father so that means that we have to spend a lot of time together. It doesn't help that my mom and his mom are best friends.

My father and mother even bought a fucking farm for him and me when we were five years old. That's where my hate for him grew.

He would always chase me around with chickens, which are my least favorite animals in the world. Every time we went to that farm, he would chase me around with them and I would always end up crying.

After that, he would show me that he hates me in other ways such as teasing me for my choice of clothing when I was a toddler and didn't have the best style, or how girls aren't as good as guys, or even drawing on my face or cutting some of my hair whenever I was asleep.

But before he started being a jackass towards me, he was actually sweet.

One of my earliest memories of Alexander and I was when he gave me a pretty flower and said that he loved me with a beautiful smile on his face. I remember how red my cheeks were that day.

But after that it's always been him teasing me, bullying me in any way he can, corrupting me even.

"Are you even listening to what I am saying?" Becca asks me with her eyebrow raised, acting like a bitch as usual.

"No Becca, please tell me what you were saying so I can pretend that I actually give a fuck," I say giving her a fake smile.

I have no clue why I am hanging out with these bimbos but sometimes they entertain me. Today, they are just being annoying which makes me want to punch them in the face.

Becca laughs and shakes her head. "You and your attitude, Thalia," she looks at me. "I was asking you about Cameron. I saw him talk to you today."

I try not to blush as I think about Cameron.

He is this guy in my history class. Today we had to work together on this study guide the teacher gave us and he gave me his number so that we could talk later about the study guide.

Cameron is cute and sweet. He always gives me such a nice and warm smile and I swear he looks like one of the gods from above.

He just moved here a couple of months ago and since then I have had my eyes on him.

I told Jane about him, my best friend who also happens to be my cousin, and she said that I should go for it, even though she doesn't even understand high school guys.

"Nothing. Cameron just gave me his-"

I feel cold liquid being poured on my head as I talk, and I can't help but scream and clench my hands into fists. I look down at my shirt and see that it is soaked with milk.

Fucking jackass.

I turn around and look up at him.

He just has this small smirk on his face as he looks down at me with mischief in his eyes.

I stand up and face him, trying to make myself look taller in front of him but it's no use.

He is the tallest guy in his grade, and I still haven't grown much from my 5'6 height.

"Fucking Xander!" I yell and put my finger on his chest. "What the hell is wrong with you? You're fucking sick!"

"I thought you knew how sick I was, Thalia," he smiles down at me, but I can't help but feel rage spread throughout my body.

"There is seriously something wrong with you."

I push him out of the way and walk past him leaving through the doors of the cafeteria.

I'm so going to get him back.

Fuck him.

Fuck his stupid smirk.

Fuck his stupid tall body.

Fuck his beautiful fucking face.

And fuck Alexander Russo.

When I am in the parking lot of the school I go to my car and unlock the door.

Technically I am not supposed to be driving but who gives a shit? My dad controls the police in the whole country, so I get to do whatever I want, plus my house is right down the street.

I see a sweater in the back, so I grab it and smell it to see if it's clean; it is.

I put it down and then lift the baseball t-shirt I'm wearing over my head and then throw it in the car.

I turn around and face my car door.

As I am about to take off my undershirt, I feel a pair of hands grab my breasts making my blood freeze and turn around.

I see an old guy with a long gray beard and wrinkles on his face.

He has to be sixty or something.

And on drugs.

I slap his face and push him away from me.

"Get the fuck off of me you weirdo," I say and I'm about to turn around, but he turns me around and pushes me against the car. "Let me fucking go," I say as I try to push him away from me.

He still holds a tight grip on one of my arms. With my other arm, I reach into my back pocket and get my hand knife. I flip it in my hand before stabbing the blade into his neck making him immediately release me and scream in pain.

I grab the knife out of his neck and push him to the floor. I stand above him and dig the knife into his chest and drag it down his body as his screams fill the air.

Thank god my car is covering us from the school cameras and I parked far too.

I take my knife out of his body and look down at him.

Fucking dickhead.

I hear slow claps from behind me which makes me turn around and see Alexander walking towards me slowly with a smirk on his face as he claps.

"Never been more impressed, angel."

Two

PRESENT

I hear my alarm go off, making me open my eyes and roll to my side to turn the alarm off.

I look at the clock from over my TV that is mounted to the wall.

6:30 am

Holy shit.

I close my eyes for another second before taking the covers off of my body and getting out of bed. I walk inside the bathroom and look in the mirror to see how horrible I look. My long dark hair is a mess and it looks like a bird's nest. Don't even get me started on the smudged mascara around my eyes.

Last night I went out on a mission to kill this one guy who was sending threats to my father, so my mom asked me to go and kill him.

It was a long night. I got in super late.

He didn't trust easily so I had to seduce him and then bring him into one of the hotels nearby to kill him. Since I had nobody with me, I had to get rid of the body myself and ship it off to his Mafia.

I didn't care where he was from, only if I got the job done and I did.

I did have to kiss him in some places I didn't want to, but you have to do what you have to do. At least he was attractive, but I don't let looks get to me.

I wash my face before getting out of the restroom and walking inside my closet to pick out my clothes for the gym.

The reason I have to wake up so early every day is that I have training in the mornings and my brother has school. My mother wants Killian to go to high school and experience that kind of thing like I did. In high school I usually stuck to myself because I never really liked to engage in all of the social events that the students held at the school. They were stupid. I had a few friends in freshman year and later on I became one of the most popular girls at my school.

Girls hated me because their boyfriends liked me better. I can't help it that I'm a flirt. It's literally my job to do that.

One of my friends, Becca, stopped being friends with me because I slept with her boyfriend. I thought they broke up and he was attractive, so I didn't say no. When she found out, she was furious and stopped talking to me.

I learned that she went to college to be a doctor while I stayed here to become the first-ever female mafia boss. To be more specific, the Italian Mafia Donna.

From my knowledge and my father's, there has never been a female heir to a mafia group since ever and lucky me, I'll be the first. My father and I argued about it, and he said he wanted Killian to take over his role since he is getting older, and he is a boy, but I reasoned with him and he eventually gave in.

He still treats me as his *la mia principessa.*

I change into a pair of leggings and a white sports bra. After I put my shoes on, I leave my room.

As I walk through the hallway, I see all of the pictures of me and my brother as toddlers and then pictures of me and Jane. I also see my mom and father's wedding pictures which always make me smile because whenever I look at them together, I actually believe that love is real and not just something that happens in stories or movies.

I walk inside the kitchen and see my brother, Killian, and my mother, cooking.

"The monster's awake," Killian mutters as he eats his breakfast that my mother made.

My brother Killian is fifteen, about to turn sixteen, soon. I thought over the years our relationship would get better, and we would stop arguing but that definitely isn't the case. If anything, he is more annoying than ever.

And when he brings his friends over, he sometimes acts like a jackass towards me. His friends are assholes though and always try to hit on me but Killian always makes sure to punch them in the face if they try to make a move but he sometimes forgets I know how to handle myself and that I basically kill people for a living.

"Bite me," I sneer as I walk past him towards the coffee machine that is next to my mother.

"Do you guys always have to argue this early in the morning?" my mother says.

My mother, Aria De Luca. Used to be Aria White but then she married my father. She was part of the American Mafia but then she and my father fell in love after she snuck into his warehouse. She has told me the story of how they met. It's honestly like one of the romance stories that people write in books. A cliché romance story.

"I have to if Killian is being a jackass all the time," I say as I make my coffee.

"Don't you have someone to kill?" Killian says and glares at me.

I look back at him. "Don't you have some homework to complete to pick up your grades?"

"Will both of you stop?" my mother says and turns to look at the both of us. "You guys always fucking argue," she mutters.

"What's going on?" I turn around and see my father walk inside the kitchen, with a suit on and his hair messy. He walks over to my mother and kisses her on the lips while also putting his hands on her hips. "Good morning, *amore*."

My father, Ace De Luca. Leader of the Italian Mafia. He is known for being cold and emotionless but around us, he just seems like a regular dad with an attitude. I know that when he is around my mom, he acts differently. His whole mood shifts into something lighter and angelic. I don't want someone to love me unless someone loves me the way my father loves my mother. My mother says that he used to be a dick when they first fell in love and when I see him around his soldiers he is a dick to them.

"Ew," Killian mutters.

He is anti-emotions about everything.

He hates everything in general.

My father removes his lips from my mother's and glares at Killian. "Don't you have school?" my father looks at the clock on the wall and then back at Killian who stops eating.

"Shit," Killian mutters before getting off the stool and running out of the kitchen.

"Don't try and fight anyone today, Killian!" my mom yells as he runs out.

I roll my eyes and continue to make my coffee, putting my favorite creamer in the coffee before taking a sip of it and sitting on the stool close to the island.

"Don't you have training? Alexander is already in the gym with Alessandro waiting for you," my dad says as he still holds my mother close to him.

I roll my eyes when he says that douche's name. "I don't understand why I have to do it with him. All he does is mess around and talk about his latest one-night stands and what he does with them," I grimace remembering all of the things he has told me.

One time he was talking about how he was banging some girl in the bathroom at a club he went to the previous night. He gave me all the details about how she felt, looked, and the things she said as he pounded into her with people nearby.

I mean I don't judge people with what they do with their hook-ups, but you don't have to go around telling people about it. If anything, you should keep those intimate details to yourself. Also, there is a limit to how many times you should whore around, and Alexander reached his limit a long time ago. I wouldn't be surprised if he has an STD.

My dad chuckles and my mother just shakes her head and sighs lightly.

"Well, you have to go today. Alessandro said that you have to come today because you are learning new techniques for using guns," my father says.

"I already know how to use a gun," I smirk.

"Doubt that," my father smirks.

My mother lets go of my father and walks over to the stove. "Do you want anything to eat before you go to the gym?"

"No, I am good, thanks," I say.

"Have you thought about your birthday at all? You're going to be turning twenty so it has to be something big," my mother says as she puts food on a plate.

"Well, Jane is coming over so I will probably hang out with her."

Jane is my best friend. Sadly, she lives in America with her father, Cole Reyes, and her mother, Layna Reyes. Cole is the second in command of the American Mafia. Jane is two years younger than me and in college trying to pursue a career as a teacher. She loves kids and wants to work with them instead of staying in the kind of business I am doing.

So, she is always at college, and I barely see her or talk to her that much anymore because she is always busy but she is finally coming over and I am so excited.

"Well, we are having dinner with the family before you go out anywhere."

"Who's coming?"

I see my father's eyes widen a little bit making me think everyone is going to be coming.

Oh god, the whole family is coming.

We have a huge family. It's hard to keep up with everyone.

"Everyone," my mother states bluntly as if it's nothing.

My mom loves seeing the family.

My dad on the other hand likes to keep to himself.

I sigh. "Why? I'm just turning twenty. It's not that big of a deal."

"Yeah but did you forget that Alexander is also turning twenty-one? Don't go thinking you're that special, Thalia," my mother chuckles.

"Oh yes, how can I forget? Our birthdays are one week apart," I say, giving her a fake smile.

Sadly, my mother had to give birth to me a week away from when Alexander was born.

Every year when it's our birthday we always have to have a party together. Most annoying shit ever because I basically have to share everything on that day with him even though it's my day. I don't mean to sound conceited but it's annoying that twenty years of my life have been consumed with Alexander and not in a good way.

I will admit I have tried to kill him a couple of times and he has tried to kill me but somehow, he always knows when I am trying to kill him, and vice versa.

"Well, for this dinner please try not to argue so much with him. I just want a nice family dinner with all of us for once," my mother says looking at me and my dad.

My dad furrows his eyebrows, "Why are you looking at me?"

"Because you always argue with Alex and it's so fucking annoying," my mother rolls her eyes.

Alex is my mother's brother. He is the leader of the American Mafia but soon his daughter Ariel is marrying her fiancé which will make him the new leader. They met during this assassin academy they went to, and I guess he and her fell madly in love and all that bullshit. But whenever my uncle Alex is here, he and my father always argue nonstop.

"It's his fault that he is a dick to me for no reason."

"Just play nice," my mother says with begging eyes that my father can never resist and then she looks at me. "Both of you."

My dad smirks at me and I just smile at him.

We both know that won't happen.

I drink the rest of my coffee and put the cup in the sink. "Whatever."

Three

"I'M HERE!" I HEAR A FAMILIAR VOICE FROM DOWN THE hall before the door of my room opens revealing Jane. I smile as she wraps her arms around me. My eyes close automatically from the amazing scent of her hair. One thing I love about Jane is how much she takes care of her hair. She kind of has to take care of her hair because of the texture and curls. "Happy birthday!" she says once she's released me from the hug.

"Thanks," I chuckle. "Where are your mom and dad?"

"Downstairs with your parents," Jane states.

"Is everyone else here yet?" I ask.

Today is the dinner with the family and also my birthday. It hasn't been that interesting. All that happened was breakfast with my mom, dad, and brother. Luckily, I didn't have to go to training because if I did then I would have to deal with Alexander and his brooding self.

My mom and dad gave me some gifts this morning. They said

they have more for me later, but I told them they didn't have to get me anything.

My mom gave me her vintage red dress from when she was my age. It was a summer dress, and it is stunning. I was thinking about wearing it tonight, but I don't want to get it dirty. I also don't think it's a club dress so if I do wear it, it will be at a family party, not a club party.

My dad gave me a freaking gun. It has my name on it. I don't know why he gave me a gun because I already have so many. I keep a stash of weapons in my closet.

"No, they are on their way. My mom, dad, and I came a little earlier than the others, so I think that your uncle's plane is landing soon. He came with your grandma," Jane states. I nod my head, making her know that I understand what she is saying. "Are you ready for tonight? What are you wearing?"

"A white corset top and a black mini skirt that I have. How is school going?"

"Decent," Jane shrugs her shoulders. "It's normal for a regular person, I guess. How is being a soon-to-be mafia boss?" Jane chuckles.

"Ehh, nothing that interesting," I shrug with a little smirk on my face.

"I haven't seen you forever and you say that nothing interesting happened while I was away?" Jane asks and raises an eyebrow at me.

I shake my head from side to side. "Nope. Just the regular mission crap and Killian being a constant dick."

"Where is your brother anyway? I didn't see him downstairs."

I roll my eyes.

Killian is out with his friends. He snuck out to go and hang out with them instead of staying for dinner. I am not going to tell mom or dad though because when they figure it out they will deal with him.

"He is out with his friends. He decided to ditch."

I saw Killian sneak out of his room through the window and when he saw me watching him, he said not to say anything, but I don't really care.

There is security everywhere, so I am shocked how he figured out how to get through it all. We have guards around the estate and then cameras everywhere, but Killian manages to sneak out every time.

For the next hour or so Jane and I just talked as I got ready for the dinner.

She told me all about this guy who is in her child development class. She said that he seems super sweet and that he is cute. I told her that she should go for it, but Jane isn't the type of girl to go after guys.

She is more of the shy type when she's around people she doesn't really know, but around me and her close friends, she is super talkative.

"Girls! Dinner is ready!" I hear my mom yell from downstairs.

I haven't gone downstairs since lunch because my mom said she wanted me to stay upstairs. I have no clue why, but I have a good guess of what she is doing.

I look at myself in the mirror one more time before leaving my room with Jane behind me. When I get downstairs, I see decorations everywhere along with my family standing there with their phones out and smiles on their faces.

"Happy Birthday!" they all yell.

I widen my eyes and look around the room. Gosh, literally everyone is here.

"Hi," I say, not knowing what else to say. "You guys really didn't have to do all this," I walk closer to them and start hugging them all one by one.

"Oh, happy birthday T," Ariel says as she hugs me first.

"Thank you, I'm so glad you're here," I say as I hug her back.

After a lot of hugging and saying 'hi' to all of the family we go and sit in the dining room, where we have an extremely long table and a chair out for everyone to sit at.

I sit down at the table along with everyone else. I sit at the head of the table in between Jane and my mother on my side.

I look at the other end of the table and see the douche-bag himself.

Alexander Russo.

On each side of him are his parents, Emma and Leo Russo.

His dark blonde hair is just freshly cut, and he is wearing a tux and all. I can see the flashy watch on his wrist and his dark hazel eyes staring into my bright green ones.

Alexander is the heir of one of the smaller mafia organizations here in Italy. His father, Leo Russo is second in command for our mafia but then my father decided to split the mafia in half so that they can both deal with different things. So essentially, he and I are both heirs to the Italian Mafia but I am more of the rightful heir then he is since my father is the boss of the Italian Mafia while Leo is just a boss for the smaller Italian Mafia, he basically still works for my father.

"I just want to say happy birthday to my daughter, Thalia," my mother says as maids start to bring in the food that the chef made. We did have a chef named Lana, but she died when I was a kid from a heart attack. "I also want to say happy early birthday to Alexander," my mother says looking at Alexander who just had a bored expression on his face.

Honestly, he is a douchebag.

I don't understand how my mother sees him as a saint but in reality, he is a fuck boy who likes to get into girls pants without even thinking another thought about it. He is arrogant in everything he does.

I have had an extreme amount of hate for him for as long as I can remember.

We would always have to spend time together because my mother and father are friends with his parents but no matter how much they try to bring us together they can't.

I have never hated anyone or used the word hate because it's a very strong word, but Alexander Russo is the one person I hate. There are so many things he has done to me such as teasing me in grade school with all of his little friends next to him, making sure to pour milk on my head at lunch in middle school, and in high school he always made sure to knock down my books.

Obviously, I wouldn't take his shit so every time he did something like that to me I would always hit him back with something worse.

It's kind of sad that we hate each other so much because we used to be good friends. But one day Alexander's mind shifted and now he hates me and makes it his sole mission to corrupt me.

"Thank you, Aria," Alexander says, showcasing a fake smile but I can tell he doesn't want to be here. "I also want to say happy birthday to my birthday twin, Thalia," Alexander looks at me and smirks.

God, I want to wipe that smirk off of his face and shove it up his-

"Aww, isn't that sweet," my grandmother says while looking between the both of us.

I try to refrain from rolling my eyes because I don't want to upset my mother.

"Thalia?" my father says, looking at me. I look up at him and raise my eyebrow. "What do you say to Alexander?"

I sigh and look at Alexander across the table.

He still has that stupid smirk on his face.

I give him a fake smile. "Thank you. Happy early birthday to you, Alexander," I say, bringing my champagne glass up, toasting, making everyone else do the same.

As Alexander drinks his champagne, he stares straight at me while glaring and I do the same.

Fuck you, Alexander Russo.

Four

Jane and I get out of the car and walk inside the club.

After dinner, Jane and I went to the club. My dad wanted me to have a driver because he wants to make sure that I get home and to the club safely, even though he knows I can handle myself.

My mom also asked me where Killian was, and I told her that I didn't know. She knew I was lying.

But I can't wait to see my mom's face when she sees Killian, especially my dad's because he will definitely be giving Killian a hard time.

As we walk inside the club, we hear music blasting through the speakers, and we see people dancing and swaying their hips side to side. The lights in the room are flashing so many different colors, making you think you were in a different world.

I had reserved a private room tonight since I invited some of my friends so that we could all hang out in there instead of worrying about getting groped by random people on the dance floor.

Jane and I walk up to the private room and there is also a security guard in front of the door. He already knows who I am, so he opens the door and then I see decorations and balloons around the entire room.

"Surprise!" my friends all say, as they put their hands in the air.

I feel a small smile come on my face. "Thank you, guys."

My friends Leila and Carson walk towards me and wrap their arms around me.

"Happy birthday, beautiful," Carson says.

"Thank you," I say and let go of them.

I look behind them and I see Cameron, Julian, and Mason.

I walk towards Julian and Mason and hug them, and they hug me back. "Happy birthday, Thalia," Mason says as he hugs me with Julian.

"Thank you. I am so happy you guys are here." I say and unwrap my arms from around them. "I missed you guys."

"Well, you are always busy so it's hard to get you to hang out with us," Julian jokes.

I give him a fake smile and look at Jane who tries to refrain from laughing.

Yea I am definitely busy but not with what he thinks.

"Yea I just have been busy with family stuff," I lie.

I feel hands on my waist making me look up and see Cameron. "Hello, baby," he says and leans down and captures my lips with his. I kiss him back and I feel his other hand slide on my waist, holding me against him. "Happy birthday, gorgeous," he mumbles against my lips.

I remove my lips from his so that we don't get too heated in front of everyone. "Thank you," I smile at him.

Cameron isn't my boyfriend.

He is more of a fuck buddy.

He and I met during our first year of high school and long story short he and I got closer throughout the years and became friends. A few months after high school is when we started messing around. I met his friends and got a little close with them and then Cameron and I started to feel an attraction with one another, and we ended up having sex one night and doing that over and over and over and over.

He says that he wants a relationship, but I don't because if I do then that will complicate things for me since I am the soon-to-be leader of my mafia and having him caught up in it all will just mess everything up.

Besides, I don't have any feelings for him. I just think he is hot and good in bed. He doesn't mind being fuck buddies but he did say that he likes me and I told him I didn't want to complicate things but we both made an agreement that we were just going to be fuck buddies and not do anything else with any other people.

Now that might be hard for me since I am a seductress and assassin, but I have to do what I have to do and what Cameron doesn't know won't hurt him. Plus, I am not fucking anyone, just kissing, that is the farthest I have ever done with anyone on a mission.

Cameron and his friends know nothing about me being in the mafia or what my job is and requires.

"How was dinner with your family?" Cameron asks, looking down at me.

"Good. We had risotto and then tiramisu."

"Sounds delicious," Cameron says with a smirk. "I have a gift for you, but you might have to wait for a few hours," Cameron whispers in my ear.

I chuckle. "Okay, let's start the party first."

The DJ in the room starts playing music making all of us dance for a little while before ordering drinks.

After many shots, we are a little tipsy while dancing. Jane and I are singing the lyrics of the song that was playing while everyone else just dances.

I don't really go out a lot with Cameron and his friends because I am always busy.

I mean, after high school I mainly focused on trying to learn how the role of being a Donna works and how to be a successful leader. I know for a fact that I will have to end things with Cameron and that I won't be able to see him anymore which I am okay with, but it sucks that I won't be able to speak to him. I just don't want to risk anything if I keep this relationship with him.

As I am dancing with the girls and Jane, I see Cameron give me a look. But it wasn't seductive or teasing, it was a look that begged me to come to him.

I walk away from the girls and go over to Cameron. "What's wrong?" I furrow my eyebrows.

He stands up from the couch. "I have to go. My mom just told me that my sister was admitted into the hospital. She fainted."

"Oh no, of course. You should go," I say while giving him a worried look. "Is she okay though?"

"Yea my mom just texted me," Cameron says looking at his

phone. "It was really bad this time, so she just wanted to take her to check and see if she was okay."

His sister has severe anxiety, so she probably fainted from a panic attack. I met his sister, and she is super sweet. She is around Killian's age, and I am pretty sure they go to the same school.

"Do you know if she is taking her medication or if it's working?"

I don't know how these kinds of things work because I have never dealt with anxiety or panic attacks.

"I don't know. That's why she is at the hospital because she hasn't had a panic attack this bad since before she started taking medication."

"Okay, well text me when you get there and let me know how she is doing," I state and wrap my arms around him. "She will be okay," I state softly.

I have a lot of sympathy for Cameron. He has been through a lot. His dad left him when he was just a kid and the last time he saw him was at his graduation and he got in a fight with him, I guess. Then he has to help his mom out since she never really does anything. I wouldn't say she is a bad mom, but she looks drained every time I see her.

"Okay," he says and let's go of me. "Happy birthday," he whispers before leaving.

Five

I join the girls on the dance floor.

I don't bother getting another drink because I don't feel like drinking anymore. Now I am just worried about Cameron's sister.

I really do hope she is okay.

As I dance with the girls I hear the door open making me turn around to see who entered.

Heat spreads throughout my body as I see Alexander, in a suit, walk in as the security holds the door for him.

I feel my mood become more annoyed than worried. Any thought of Cameron and his sister goes out the window once I make eye contact with *him*.

Of course, he is here. He is always everywhere I am just so he can come in and ruin things.

After dinner, I don't know where Alexander went. Jane and I just left as soon as we could, and I didn't pay any mind to Alexander and what he was doing. My mother did ask me if I could take him with me the night before since she knew Jane and I were going out, but I told her that I didn't want to.

My mom and dad know how I feel about him. I hate him.

I see Jane look at Alexander from across the hall and then back at me with a smirk.

I roll my eyes at her before walking towards Alexander who is raising his eyebrow at me, leaning against the wall near the door.

"What are you doing here?" I ask once I am right in front of him.

"Just making sure the birthday girl isn't doing anything embarrassing. Wouldn't want to ruin your reputation now, would you, Thalia?"

I can't help but roll my eyes at the way my name rolls off his tongue smoothly.

God just his presence being this close to me is making me want to slap him in the face.

I put on a fake smile. "Aww, it's nice to see that you care for me, Alexander. If anything, I think you might have a little crush on me."

"Sure, angel," Alexander chuckles.

"Don't you have some girl to screw? Why are you here?" I sneer.

"I was hoping you would be that girl, Thalia," Alexander says in a low voice with a smirk.

I chuckle and walk closer to him. Alexander puts his hands on my hips once my chest is against his.

I feel hot getting this close to him but it's probably because I hate his hands on me. But with Alexander, it's in his blood to touch anything with boobs or a pussy.

I lean closer to his ear and kiss under it. "You have better luck getting a guy to fuck you rather than me. Sorry, Russo, but I have standards."

"Oh, is that a challenge, angel?" Alexander raises his eyebrow at me, and his face seems to lean closer to mine.

My eyes automatically go to his lips, soft smooth lips.

He still has his hands on my hips making me grit my teeth.

I lean away from him a little, so we have at least some distance between us. "Alexander, if you don't get your hands off of me, I will make sure to skin them while you're sleeping in the black silk sheets on your bed," I say in a low voice while glaring at him.

"Are you offering to get in bed with me, Thalia?" he smirks while looking down at me.

God that stupid fucking smirk.

"Do you only think with your dick, Xander?" I ask while using the one nickname he hates.

For some weird reason, he hates that nickname. Ever since I used it in grade school, he always got mad at me when I used it. I think it's because kids would laugh or make fun of him.

Alexander clenches his jaw but before he can say anything we hear gunshots go off and people screaming from downstairs.

My body stays alert and I get Alexander's hands off of me.

The door next to us opens and I see the security guard come in. "Miss De Luca, there is a problem outside."

I walk towards him. "No shit." I glare at him and roll my eyes. "Take these guys home," I say pointing to everyone who is still dancing except for Jane who has a scared look on her face.

I was hoping she wouldn't hear but she hears everything and is always on alert.

"And you, Miss De Luca?"

"Don't worry about me," I say before walking over to Jane. "Go home. Tell my mom and dad about what happened. I'm going to go see what's going on." I tell Jane as I hear more gunshots from outside.

"No, just come home Thalia," Jane says in a scared tone.

I can tell she is scared. She isn't fit for this kind of life.

"I will be okay," I assure her. "Go with him. He is going to take you guys home. I need to see what's happening." I hear more gunshots go off making me walk away from Jane and past the security who is just waiting at the door, but I look at him and say "Don't just fucking stand there, idiot, get them home," I say pointing to my friends who are so oblivious except for Jane.

I walk past him and grab his gun that is strapped to his belt.

Should have listened to my father when he said to bring a gun.

I check to see if there are any bullets in the magazine. There are so I pop it back in and walk out of the hallway to see what all the screaming and shooting is about.

When I walk out of the corner, I see the whole club a mess and then some men walking around scoping the place. There are a lot of dead bodies on the floor and tables flipped over.

Thank god there is a back door from the VIP area for Jane and the others to leave.

"Where the fuck is she? Vladimir said she would be here," one of the guys says but I don't do anything.

I just stand there listening to their conversation. "Keep checking. She should be here," the other one says.

I walk a little closer making the wooden floor under me creak.

I see all of the men stop what they are doing and look in my direction.

I open my mouth and step away only to feel an arm wrap around me and a hand cover my mouth. I feel panic spread through my body.

"Shhh," I hear a familiar voice say as my back is pressed against a strong body. "It's me, angel," Alexander whispers and I feel his lips touch my ear sending chills down my body.

"Hey, I think I heard something over here!" one of the guys says and I hear footsteps coming closer.

Alexander takes his hand off of my mouth and puts his hand on my waist.

"What's happening?" I whisper.

"I don't know."

"What do we do?"

"Watch and learn, angel. All of those training sessions you missed might have helped with these kinds of situations," Alexander says before taking his hands off of me.

"Alex-"

Alexander walks out of the corner. "What the fuck is going on over here?" Alexander says while walking more out of the little area we were hiding in. "Damn, I think I was dancing with that one."

I can't help but roll my eyes.

I hear guns click making me think they aimed their guns at him.

"Who are you?" one of the men asks but he has a deeper voice.

"Bitch, I am Alexander Russo," Alexander says making me shake my head.

He is so fucking stupid.

"You're coming with us," one of them says.

I peek out of the hiding spot and see Alexander's back and then all of the men pointing their guns at him.

I know for a fact Alexander has a stupid smirk on his face.

"See, I can't do that," Alexander says and he walks towards them. "I have a lovely friend that I need to take home. It's her birthday so she had a little too much to drink."

I can't help but roll my eyes at Alexander again.

"Not happening. You're coming with us," one of the men steps towards Alexander but then I see Alexander grab his gun from his waistband and shoot that guy in the head before roundhouse kicking another one.

God, he can't fight all of them off on his own.

Without thinking I come out of my hiding space and start shooting bullets at all of the guys in front of me.

Alexander and I keep shooting at the guys.

I shoot one of the guy's hands making him wince and drop his gun to the floor. I knock him out by hitting him in the head with my gun. He falls limp to the floor; I turn to look at Alexander and see him shoot one more guy before bringing his gun down.

"Shit," he sighs while looking at all of the dead bodies.

"What the fuck is going on?" I say while looking around the room that is filled with dead bodies.

Six

I called some of my father's men so that they could get rid of the bodies at the club.

It was a lot.

Alexander and I rode in his car, and we also had to bring the unconscious body, that I knocked out, in the trunk. He was pissed off. After all, he didn't want to dirty his car with the unconscious body because he had some blood on his forehead. Alexander didn't want blood on the white seats of his fancy Ferrari, so we had put him in the trunk.

Once we got to the estate, Alexander parked the car and we both got out. He grabbed the body from the back of the car.

"Do you mind doing some work?" Alexander says as we walk to the front door.

"I am not the one who made the first move to get him. You did," I say before opening the front door.

"They're here!" I hear Jane yell. I see her run towards me, and she wraps her arms around me. "Oh my god, thank god you're okay."

"Jane, I am fine," I say while letting go of her. "Where are my mom and dad?"

"In the office with Leo and Emma."

I nod my head and turn to look at Alexander. "Just put the body in one of the cells downstairs. You know the way," I say before walking to where the office is.

None of the family is here right now because they are staying at the guest house. My father thought that since my mother has such a big family, whenever they come to visit, they can stay in the guest house that my father made.

It has a few rooms for everyone because my dad says that he likes his personal space so that is why he made a separate house for them to stay in. But we have a lot of guest rooms here as well.

I walk into my father's office without knocking and I see both Alexander's parents, Leo and Emma, and my parents.

My father is sitting in his chair while my mother is pacing back and forth behind him while looking down. Emma is sitting in a chair and then Leo is standing next to my father looking down at papers on his desk.

I close the door making them all look at me.

My mom looks at me and she walks towards me and wraps her arms around me. "Oh my god, Thalia. Are you okay?" my mom pulls away to look at my face and she puts her hands on my face making sure I am okay.

"I'm fine, mom," I say, taking her hands off of my face and holding them in my hands. "I am okay."

"Where is Alexander?" Emma asks, standing up from her seat.

"He is-"

"Right here," I hear Alexander say as he walks inside the office. I turn around and see he has some blood on his white dress shirt and his hands are also bruised. "I had to get some info," Alexander states.

I turn my head and ignore how hot my face feels.

Emma walks towards him and she hugs him. "Oh, I'm so glad you're okay."

"I'm fine ma, don't worry," Alexander states as he lets his mother hug him.

My mom walks to my father's side, and I sit down in front of my father in one of the chairs. Emma sits down on the couch on the right of the office and then Alexander sits down next to me.

I look down at his hands. "You should clean that. It will get infected."

"No shit, Sherlock," Alexander mutters but he just looks at my father who is looking through papers.

"Thalia, want to explain to me why Jane ran into my office telling me that you were about to die?" my dad says as he looks up at me.

"You're asking as if it's my fault," I say, sounding offended. "I don't even know what happened. I was talking to Alexander and then we both heard gunshots. Alexander and I killed all of the gunmen except one."

"What did these men look like?" my dad asks, looking between Alexander and me.

"They are Russian," Alexander states bluntly. "I interrogated one of the guys that Thalia knocked out. He is in the cell, still alive, but he is kind of weak and a little roughed up."

"What did he say?" My father asks, leaning over his desk staring at Alexander.

"Know a guy named Vladimir?"

"Last name?"

"Uh, Ivanov."

I see my father's jaw clench and my mother look at him with a shocked expression on her face.

My mother then looks at Alexander. "Are you sure his last name is Ivanov?"

"Yea that is what the guy said. I also undressed him and found a tattoo. It was similar to the Russian tattoo from twenty years ago, but it is different in some aspects," Alexander pulls out his phone and shows my dad a picture of what I am guessing is the Russian tattoo.

"Shit," my father mutters. He looks up at my mother. "That's not possible, is it?"

"Ace, you said that Dimitri didn't have any children," my mother claims.

I furrow my eyebrows.

Dimitri Ivanov was the Russian Mafia Leader, but my father killed him and his entire family. My mother told me the story. My mother said that he was positive that there were no heirs, but I guess he was wrong.

"*Cazzo*!" my father mutters before going on his computer and typing some things. "Did that guy in the cell say anything else, Alexander?"

"Not really. I didn't do much damage to him because I thought that you would want to handle him too," Alexander shrugs. "But he said something about the wait being over, whatever that means."

I see my father sigh.

Why does he look so scared? I have never seen my father this scared or worried or threatened before.

"Dad, what's wrong?" I ask.

"Go to your room. We will discuss this matter in the morning. Alexander, you take one of the guest bedrooms."

I refrain from asking him what's really wrong and instead I follow Alexander out the door.

Seven

ARIA

Thalia and Alexander walk out the door and I hear them both arguing as they walk further down the hallway.

They never know how to get along.

I let out a sigh and rub my temple while pacing back and forth again.

"What do we do? I thought we handled this twenty years ago?" Leo asks, looking at Ace.

I hear Ace let out an annoyed sigh. "I fucking did."

"Then how the hell is there an Ivanov still breathing?"

"I don't fucking know, Leo," Ace sighs and takes a deep breath. "Meet me in the cells downstairs." Leo and Emma both make a move to leave the office making it just Ace and me. Ace stands up from his chair and runs his fingers through his dark hair. "Fucking Russians," Ace yells as he punches a wall.

God, he still has anger issues after the twenty-one years I have known him.

I walk towards Ace and stand in front of him. "It's okay. We will take care of them," I say assuringly.

"Ari, I thought I fucking got him. I thought I fucking killed them. All of them."

I put my hands on his face and stroke his cheek. "It's fine. We will handle this. We will fix this. It will be okay."

The past twenty years have been amazing with Ace. It's been nothing but a dream. Ace was a total asshole but then he and I fell in love and everything between us has been euphoric. There have definitely been ups and downs like having Dante ruining our lives and Ace's mom dying but life goes on.

I still haven't told Ace about the recent news I got from the doctors the other day. But I know it's going to break him to pieces.

Ace let out another sigh. "Okay. Let's just see what this Russian scum wants," Ace kisses the top of my head.

We both leave his office and meet Leo and Emma downstairs who are talking. We don't see Jane, Thalia, or Alexander in the living room, so I am guessing that they are in their rooms.

"Okay, so what are we doing?" Leo asks as we walk down the hallway of cells.

"What Aria can do best. Get the information we need out of him and then we come up with a solution." We get to the cell where the man is, and Ace and I walk inside while Leo and Emma stand outside of the cell and just watch. "Do your thing, *amore*," Ace states and I walk closer to the man.

He definitely looks roughed up from when Alexander beat him. But he is still conscious.

Sadly, he is wearing nothing but thin black boxers.

Thank god he is wearing just boxers though because it's always fucking disgusting when I see men's dick's other than Ace's.

I lean towards him, making the man look up at me. "I feel bad for you," I state while observing his face. It showcases fear, especially when he looks at Ace behind me. "My daughter left you alive while she and Alexander killed off the rest."

This man looked young. Probably a little older than Thalia.

"Please just kill me," the man begs.

"Oh, trust me I will but first I need to know some things," I grab the knife I keep in the back pocket of my jeans. "If you answer my questions then you will get a quick and painless death but if you make this hard then I will make sure to skin your body while you just scream in pain and beg me to kill you. So, are we doing this the hard way or the easy way?" I ask while trailing my knife down his cheek. "What's your name?"

"R-Rasputin," he stutters.

"Okay, Rasputin. Who is Vladimir Ivanov?"

"He- he is D-Dimitri's heir."

"Dimitri had an heir? Why didn't anyone know of this?"

"He has kept it a secret. He made Vladimir move somewhere else in Russia and made sure no one knew who he was or that he was the heir."

I look back at Ace, but he just looks confused and is furrowing his eyebrows while staring at Rasputin.

"What does Vladimir want?" I ask, turning my head back at Rasputin.

"He wants revenge. He wants to kill all of you," Rasputin says while trying to not make any eye contact with me. "You deserve it though. You killed them. All of them."

I stab Rasputin's shoulder making him scream out in pain. "I don't care what we deserve or did. Where is Vladimir?"

"Russia, you cunt," Rasputin spits.

Ace comes up from behind me and he punches Rasputin in the face and holds his face so that Rasputin is looking directly at Ace.

"Call my wife a cunt again and I will punch you until you can't breathe anymore. *Capito*?" Since Rasputin doesn't answer Ace punches him again. "Do you fucking understand?!" Ace yells in his face.

"Fuck you! You are all going to die anyway!" he yells as tears run down his face.

Ace shakes his head lightly before leaving the cage.

"You better pray," I state and walk closer to him before stabbing his eye. "He is going to send you straight to hell," I say as he whimpers in pain, cussing me out.

Ace comes back a few seconds later and I see him with a flame gun in his hand and a bottle of alcohol.

Ace pours the alcohol all over Rasputin's body as Rasputin yells and cusses us out over and over again. Ace smashes the glass bottle on his head making it break. Then Ace positions the flame gun at Rasputin's body before turning it on and making his whole body light up.

"Saluta satana da parte mia."

We watch Rasputin's body burn in the flames as he screams for mercy and begs to be put out of his misery

Ace has his men come and clean up the body so that he can send it to Russia as Leo, Emma, and I follow him out of the downstairs area.

Once we are back in his office, we all sit down. Ace in his seat, Emma and Leo in the seats in front of his desk, and then me behind him trying to think of a plan.

"What are we going to do? We have no clue what Vladimir is like," Leo says.

"He's right," I say, agreeing with Leo.

Ace then looks up from his desk. "I have an idea, but they won't like it," he states, making me furrow my eyebrows.

"What? Who?" I say looking down at Ace.

"The kids. They won't like it but it's the only thing I can think of right now."

"What is it?"

Ace looks up at me and sighs.

Eight

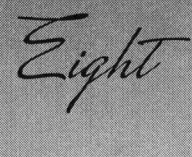

I walk inside the kitchen and I see Killian already sitting down on one of the stools that are pushed into the island.

"Thanks for not telling."

I look at Killian, shocked.

He never says thank you or anything remotely close to that.

"For what?" I raise my eyebrow.

"For not snitching."

I turn and walk to the coffee machine, starting to make my coffee. "I'm no snitch," I state coldly. "Besides I knew that mom and dad would find out, so I just said I didn't know anything."

"Yea I know. Mom told me."

"How long are you grounded for?" I ask as I pour the creamer into my coffee.

"Ehh, they haven't decided on a punishment yet. I got back in last night before Jane came in so they kind of got sidetracked by your situation. Thanks for that too by the way."

I chuckle and turn to look at him. "Well, I have a meeting with mom, dad, Leo, and Emma today. We have to talk about the Russian problem."

Killian furrowed his eyebrows. "Russians? I thought they handled that?"

"They did but I guess they didn't kill all of them. Alexander got information from this Russian we knocked out the other day."

"See what kind of shit I miss out on when I am busy with school or doing normal people things."

I take a sip of my coffee. "You haven't even had your first kill yet either. I had mine when I was around your age. Maybe a little younger."

"What was your first kill like?" Killian asks but before I can answer I hear that dreadful voice.

"Oh, I remember," I turn my head and see Alexander strolling in the kitchen with a pair of black boxer briefs on. I look at his sculpted chest and abdomen that has black ink everywhere. I notice he got some new tattoos like the snake on one of his pecs and roman numerals on his collarbone. I also see the tattoo all of our mafia members have. It is an ace card with a knife stabbed into it. My dad told me the story of the tattoo.

He has this specific tattoo design because it represents him and my mom's love. It represents how my mom inserted herself into his life even though he tried to push her away so many times.

I love the story of how they met. It was traumatic but what do you expect?

"Done staring, angel?"

I am not going to lie and say that Alexander isn't hot, because he is. He is hot as shit, probably one of the most attractive guys I know but his personality is the problem. He is a douchebag and will literally fuck anything with a pussy, no matter what. He thinks he is better than everyone else and that the world revolves around him.

I look up to meet Alexander's eyes. "When did you get those tattoos?" I take another sip of my coffee.

He looks down at the snake on his pec. "A few days ago," he shrugs.

"What was Thalia's first kill like?" Killian asks, looking at Alexander.

Alexander leans against the counter behind him and folds his arms over his chest. "Ahhh little Thalia and her first-ever kill," Alexander looks at me and he has an amused smile on his face. "Who could ever forget that terrific moment?"

"Jackass," I mumble as I take another sip of my coffee.

"Thalia was like fifteen. I remember she had her hair in a cute high ponytail she would always have her hair in." Alexander narrows his eyes at me. "She was wearing blue jeans with a baseball t-shirt."

"Get to the point," Killian says, rolling his eyes.

Alexander sighs. "We were both at school and-"

"And Alexander decided to be a dick and he poured milk all over my head, so I had to go and change my clothes since I was only wearing a white tank top underneath and I didn't want to have everyone in the school look at me and see through the tank top," I say finishing his sentence.

"That's a sight I'm willing to see," Alexander mumbles but we both hear.

"Eww, I asked what Thalia did for her first kill. Not if you would want to see her tits or not."

I roll my eyes.

"Well, I ran after Thalia to go make sure she was okay-"

I turn to look at him. "You are such a fucking liar. You went to come and find me so you could bug me. Don't fucking spin the truth."

"Anyways, I went to go look for Thalia, and instead of seeing Thalia in a white little tank top I saw her standing above a man who was like, twice her size with blood coming out of his neck and a silver blade stabbed into the side of his neck."

Killian widens his eyes. "At fifteen? Why did you even kill the guy?"

"I took off my baseball t-shirt and I was left in my tank top so that I could change into a sweater and when I was doing that some random guy from the street was stalking towards me started to touch me and shit so I took the knife I had in my pocket and killed him," I shrug.

My mom and dad always made me and Killian carry around some sort of weapon when we went places. They just wanted to make sure we were okay.

"Yup, my little angel wasn't looking very innocent that day. I think after that you started to become hotter and more badass, Thalia."

Killian grimaces. "Okay well on that note I need to go. I have school in a few minutes and you guys have your own thing to deal with," Killian says before leaving the kitchen.

I take a sip of my coffee and put it on the counter. "Yeah well, you are still the same dick since our fifth birthday when my dad got us that little farm on the hill," I say, giving him a fake smile.

When it was my fifth birthday my parents and Alexander's parents got us a farm where there were different farm animals.

A day after our fifth birthday, Alexander decided to start being a little shit to me.

The next day after our birthday, Emma took us to the farm and Alexander knew how much I hated birds so he decided it would be fun to chase me around with a chicken in his hand and then corner me inside a chicken pen. That is when my hatred for Alexander started and then he just kept being a little dick to me throughout the years.

"Oh, that's right, little Thalia was afraid of birds," Alexander chuckles. "What made you so afraid of them, Thalia?"

"Maybe because they looked like you, Xander," I mutter before passing him, while also making contact with his bare shoulder.

I feel him grab my wrist and he turns us around so that I am pushed up against the counter and he is right in front of me.

"You really know how to piss me off don't you," Alexander says in a husky voice as he looks down at me.

"Just stating facts," I shrug my shoulders and Alexander leans closer to me so that we are now chest to chest.

"Thalia, if that were true you would be running away from me right now instead of having your chest right against mine, making me feel your hard nipples through your thin ass little tank top that you wear around the house, not caring who sees," Alexander whispers in my ear. "Now tell me, am I wrong?"

I look up at Alexander and see him staring straight down at me with those gorgeous hazel eyes.

I have no clue what to say. I feel goosebumps spread through my body and chills go down my spine. I also feel a tingling feeling in my nipple area that I don't think I have felt before.

What the fuck.

Before I can fight against him or utter another word, I hear someone walking towards the kitchen making me push Alexander away from me.

"Oh good, you guys are up," Emma exclaims as she walks inside the kitchen staring between Alexander and me. "We need to talk."

Nine

"Okay, so we got more information out of that Russian hostage from yesterday-"

"We could have gotten more but your father decided to kill him because he let a few comments get to him," my mom says, cutting my dad off.

"What did he say?"

I see my dad's jaw clench. "Doesn't matter. But we have a few things we need to discuss with the both of you."

"Okay, what is it?"

Alexander and I are in my father's office. Alexander put on some clothes, and I put a sweater over my tank top because of what Alexander said in the kitchen. He chuckled when he saw I put on a sweater, covering my tank top where you could surely see my nipples through my shirt.

But I mean, I didn't really care. It's my house and as long as I am comfortable then that's all that matters.

"Well, we found out that there is a new Russian leader. His name is Vladimir Ivanov as Alexander said yesterday," Leo explains as he stands next to my father.

"He is the son of Dimitri Ivanov, but your father killed his whole family and blew up their estate," my mom explains while she sits on his lap.

That was a stupid move.

Just because he blew up their estate doesn't mean that they are actually dead. They could have had family outside of Russia.

"But obviously we didn't know that Dimitri had an heir, which is Vladimir. Vladimir was born in Saint Petersburg which is over four hundred miles away from Moscow which is far from the Ivanov estate," Leo explains.

"How did you find out all of this information?" Alexander asks.

"I had done some research and also found out that Vladimir was still in one of the major cities in Russia, so it wasn't hard to lessen the search," Leo states. "But that's not the point."

"The point is that Vladimir is out for revenge. He wants to grieve over the loss of his father and the only way he wants to do that is by killing all of us. He brought those men from last night to the club so that he could bring you two to him," my father explains pointing to Alexander and me.

"How did he know we would be there last night?"

"I don't know. I suppose we have a mole so today I will be doing a soldier check and make sure that everything is in order."

"Okay, and what do you need us to do?" Alexander asks.

I see my parents and Alexander's parents all make eye contact.

I furrow my eyebrows and look at Alexander who is observing all of them.

"What?" I mutter and then they look away from each other and look at the two of us.

"Now you both aren't going to like this but-"

"Like what, Ma?" Alexander cuts her off.

"It's what we have to do in order to make things look normal like we aren't worrying about them, or we are just not making any moves. It will buy us time to think of a strong plan to take them down and also it will make us stronger if we combine our mafia again," Aria explains.

"Okay? So, we combine them. Easy," I shrug.

"Not really," Alexander mumbles, making me look at him.

"In order to combine both mafias, there needs to be a marriage," Emma explains.

I look at Alexander and look back at my dad.

They better not be saying what I think they are saying. I look back at Alexander and see his jaw was clenched.

"We want Alexander and you to marry," my dad states bluntly.

"No," I state without thinking. "Absolutely not. No."

"Look it won't even be-"

"No, dad! I am not marrying Alexander. No offense but I don't want to be stuck with Alexander for the rest of my life," I look at my dad. "You promised me that I would be in charge of the empire someday, but I can't do that if I marry Alexander. You promised."

"I know *la mia principessa* but this is the way things have to be," my dad says in a gentle tone.

"I am not marrying him," I say while looking at Alexander with disgust. "Why would I want to marry someone who fucks different people on a daily basis. He is a jackass and only cares about himself. He is never capable of being kind to anyone unless he needs them. He thinks the entire world revolves around him," I say while pointing to Alexander.

"Like you're miss perfect," Alexander scoffs and I look at him. "You are always bitchy and always have something to complain about. You are the one who thinks that the world revolves around them, not me, angel."

"And there you go using that stupid nickname," I glare at him. "You always piss me off and you do it on purpose."

"You are the one who always has to pick a fight with me and throw those snarky little fucking looks at me when I don't do shit. You also think you are a little miss perfect, and you always think you are right about everything when really you aren't."

"Stop it both of you!" my dad yells, making me look at him. "This is happening. Whether you like it or not. I don't care what both of you think or say, this is happening. Sorry if you had other relationships but those need to be cut off. You are both going to be having this marriage and I don't want to hear any complaints about this 'cause so help me God, I will leave you both to die if it means I have to go through this headache."

"Dad-"

"No," my father cuts me off. "I don't want to hear it, Thalia. I don't care. You hear me?"

It's hard not to when he is yelling.

I roll my eyes and bite my lip to try and not to talk back to him. "I'll be in my room." I stand up from my chair and walk towards the door.

"Thalia-"

"Let her cool down, Ace," my mother says right before I walk out of the office door.

Ten

Thalia storms out of the office leaving just me sitting in the chair staring at our parents who looked stressed out.

God, I hate her sometimes.

There is just something about her that makes every single cell in my body burn.

I want her to crumble and just hurt the way she hurt me when we were five. I want her to suffer.

Thalia De Luca. God, that girl makes me want to go crazy in both good and bad ways.

Good, because it makes me feel good and my cock twitches for some reason. Bad, because I am thinking like that when I don't want to. Even more so because she is someone who messes with my head and likes to play around with me.

I used to like her a lot when we were kids but now, she just frustrates the fuck out of me, especially after what happened when she left me on the hill on my sixth birthday and her fifth birthday.

She makes my mind dizzy and she makes me want to do things irrationally. She makes me fucking think irrationally.

"I'm sorry Alexander. Thalia just-"

"I don't care." I stand up from my chair and cut Aria off. "I'm going home," I say, looking at my mother and father. "See you around," I say before walking to the office door and leaving.

Once I get outside of their house I walk to my car while also texting Alina on my phone.

Be at mine in ten. Don't be late.

I get inside my car and put my phone in my pocket before starting the car and driving out of the De Luca estate and towards my house.

Thalia Fucking De Luca.

She makes my blood boil.

She used to be so fucking innocent and never got in any trouble. I was always jealous of her because of how good and amazing she was at everything. Training, fighting, shooting, etc. But now I am better, but it didn't happen overnight.

Thalia and I have always competed against each other but for some reason, it gives me satisfaction seeing her so mad when I do things better than her or just when I get her mad in general.

Seeing her face get flustered when I am close to her makes me feel heat go down to my cock and I always need to find a release after every fucking encounter with her. No matter what happens, and it fucking frustrates me.

I feel my breathing pick up as I drive through the streets.

When I see no cars in the way I pick up the speed making it go to seventy.

Eighty.

Ninety.

Then one hundred.

Thalia Fucking De Luca.

Once I get to my house, I see Alina's car parked outside my house with her inside. But as I pull into my garage, right where all of my other cars are I see her get out.

She is wearing a skimpy-ass outfit. A white corset top making her boobs pop out and then tiny little blue shorts that show most of her ass. Let's not forget about the fucking red heels either because if Alina doesn't wear red heels is she even Alina?

I get out of my car and slam the door. I close the garage doors and walk towards Alina.

"Hey, baby," she says, trying to sound flirty but it was just fucking annoying.

Alina is a good fuck but not good company. She has amazing boobs and a decent ass, but her personality is just fucking annoying. Her voice makes me want to scream and not in a good way. She doesn't moan like a normal person either, it always has to be dramatic.

I met her in my last year of high school. She had a good body and was willing to give herself to me, so I took advantage of that. Wish I would have known if she was going to be fucking clingy or not.

"Shut the fuck up," I mutter as I walk past her and go inside the house. "You are here for one thing and one thing only."

Alina follows me all the way up to my room and once we get inside, she takes off her top while I take off my shirt.

Alina stands in front of me with her tits out and her eyes wide as she watches me. I raise my eyebrow at her and she just gets on her knees in front of me and starts undoing my belt. Once my cock is out, she starts stroking before putting her lips on the tip.

She starts teasing the fuck out of my tip making me more annoyed.

I sigh and grab her head, forcing her to take all of me in her mouth. She starts going up and down as I wrap my hand into her hair and start to thrust in her.

All I see is Thalia and her fucking see-through tank top where I saw her nipples poking through. Then her gorgeous full lips that I always imagine wrapping around me.

I move back and forth repeatedly until I spill my cum inside her mouth.

"Fuck," I sigh. I pull out of her mouth and then walk away from her. "Leave. I don't ever want to see you again," I state coldly.

"But-"

I turn to look at her. "Do I have to repeat myself?"

Alina then stands up and picks up her clothes before leaving the room.

Fuck you, Thalia De Luca.

Eleven

"Mom!" I yell as I run down the stairs.

"In the living room!" I hear her yell back.

Once I get to the last step I go to where the living room is, and I see my mom and dad both sitting on the couch with a blanket over their legs and her cuddled up to my dad's chest.

Both of their heads turn to look at me and I see my father furrow his eyebrows as he looks at my clothing. "Where are you going?"

"Out with some friends. Just wanted to let you guys know that I was heading out."

It's been a few days since the meeting we had. Things have been tense but when has it ever not been tense in this house?

"You're not going anywhere, especially dressed like that," my dad says, making me look down at my outfit.

I am wearing a skin-tight black dress with diamond spaghetti straps. The dress ends at my mid-thighs, and I am also wearing black strappy heels.

"What's wrong with what I am wearing?" I ask looking between my mom and dad.

"Thalia you aren't going outside dressed like that. Over my dead fucking body," my dad spits. "You really think I want men who are twice your age staring at you, thinking about fucking you in the alley? Hell no."

"Ace, it's just a dress. Plus Thalia knows how to handle herself, remember?" My mom raises her eyebrow at my dad and his face seems to soften a little bit when he looks down at her.

I swear she always puts him in a good mood and can make him feel better.

"Ari, I don't want her dressed like that."

"But-" I start.

"Plus, you're grounded," my dad looks up at me as I widen my eyes.

The last time I checked, I was an adult.

"Grounded?" I repeat.

"Yes."

"Why am I grounded?"

"Because of what you did the other day in the office. I don't know who you think you are, Thalia, but I won't let anyone disrespect me like that, especially my daughter. And what you said yesterday about Alexander was just unnecessary. Let me remind you that you also said it in front of Leo and Emma."

"He said shit too," I argue. "And did you even find a punishment for your son? That one who snuck out?"

"Don't worry about your brother, Thalia. We aren't talking

about him," my dad says, dismissing the subject about my brother. "You aren't going anywhere. Last time I checked you are living in my house so once you move out then you can do whatever the fuck you want, Thalia, but until then you listen to me." I scoff and look at my mom but before I can ask her my dad speaks up again. "And if you try to bring your mom in this, I'll stop you right now. Go to your room, Thalia."

I turn around and start heading to the front door. My father won't even know if I leave or not because he can't see the entrance of the front door from where he and my mom are in the living room.

I open the front door and close it before walking down the front steps and heading towards my car. Once I get inside, I start the car and then pull out of the estate after going through the security.

They are just mad that I don't want to go through with their stupid plan.

They should know that I wouldn't want to go through with it. They know how much I despise Alexander.

The day I marry Alexander is the day I go blind.

I pull up to the restaurant and get out, giving the key to the valet guy. I walk inside the restaurant and look around for Cameron.

Cameron said that he wanted to take me out to dinner, and I would never refuse dinner. He always has the best taste in food. He also wanted to spend time with me since we didn't hang out the night of my birthday.

I see him sitting down at a table with a chair in front of him.

He is wearing a white dress shirt and his hair is also styled. He looks good.

I walk towards his table, and he sees me walking so he stands up and we hug each other, and he kisses me on my cheek.

"You look beautiful as always, Thalia," Cameron says before letting me go.

I take a seat from the chair across from him and he sits down in his seat. "Thank you. You look great as well," I say and give him a wink. "Have you ordered yet?"

"No, I was waiting for you."

"Sorry if I took long. I got held up with my parents," I say while rolling my eyes.

"Yea I know how it feels. Glad I moved out but they still bug."

"I love my parents don't get me wrong, and I am thankful for everything they have done for me but sometimes they can be so frustrating."

"You should move out," Cameron suggested.

"If only it was that easy," I mutter before picking up the menu and looking through all of the options.

They have a lot of good options. I have been to this restaurant a couple of times. They have really good food choices.

"Are you guys ready to order?" the waitress says.

Cameron and I both order our food, and we give our menus to her. She says that the food will be here in less than twenty minutes which is great because I am starving.

"So how is your sister? Is she still in the hospital?" I ask.

"No, she is at home now. But the doctor put her on new medication because I guess her body wasn't reacting to the medication she was taking before."

"How is your mom?"

"She is the same as always," Cameron shrugs his shoulders "But enough about me. How was your birthday? Did you guys have fun?"

My birthday was interesting.

I almost died from Russian assassins and then I later found out I have to have an arranged marriage to the person I hate the most in the world.

Same old, same old.

"It was good. We all had fun, but the club had to kick everyone out because of some trouble that someone caused," I lie. "But it was fun. It was a pretty good day. But I wished you stayed longer."

Honestly, I'm glad he didn't because if he did then he would probably have ended up dead.

"Yes, I know and I'm sorry."

"No, it's better that you went to your sister. She needed you."

The waitress soon came back with the food; I ordered spaghetti and meatballs.

The meatballs look really fucking good.

Cameron and I both talk about different things and while he is talking, I feel my phone vibrate from inside my purse.

I take it out and look down at the screen, I see Alexander's name flash across the screen while it is still vibrating in my hand. I roll my eyes and press the power button, making the phone stop vibrating. After a few seconds, it vibrates again, and I look at my phone and see his name again.

I look up at Cameron. "Can you give me a minute?" I ask Cameron. "I need to take this call."

"Of course," Cameron nods his head, and I stand up and walk away with the phone.

"What?" I hiss once I answer.

"Where are you?" I hear Alexander say from the other side of the phone.

"Don't worry about it? Why are you blowing up my phone?"

"You need to get here. Now."

I feel panic flood through my body. "Why?"

"Do you have your car, or did you take a driver?" Alexander asks, ignoring my question.

"My car."

"Okay, get here as soon as you can."

Twelve

I told Cameron I had to leave early. I am pretty sure he wanted us to go to his place and hang out, but I obviously had other plans.

I pull up to the estate and park my car in one of the garages, next to all of the other cars. I get out and run to the front door while holding my heels and my purse in my hands.

I took my shoes off right after I got inside the car. I had to be quick and get to the house and I couldn't drive as fast as I usually drive with four-inch heels.

I open the front door and I hear talking from the kitchen making me walk further and further down the hall.

Once I get inside the kitchen I see my parents, Alexander, Alexander's parents, and my uncles Alex and Cole all standing around the kitchen island.

My father's fist is clenched, and he looks pissed off. My mother looked stressed out and worried just like everyone else in the kitchen.

God, what the fuck happened to them.

"What's wrong?" I ask, walking closer to them.

"Are you fucking crazy?!" my father says but my mother stops him.

"Not now, Ace. We need to talk about the issue at hand."

I walk fully inside the kitchen and stand next to Alexander. "What's going on?" I whisper.

"Shut the fuck up and listen and then maybe you will know," Alexander mumbles.

God, why is he in such a pissed off mood?

Asshole.

"Thalia, I will deal with you later but for now we have a problem. A big one."

"What happened?" I ask.

I feel anxiety throughout my entire body and my heart starts beating faster.

"We finally found the mole and after a long interrogation we found some information," my uncle Alex states.

"What did you find out?" I ask.

"Well, supposedly the mole was suppose to go back to Russia this weekend and he was going to deliver information to one of Vladmir's men about what is going on here. Usually, the mole would pick up a phone and call them but they knew that we knew about Russians so he was going to escape," my mom says.

"But we have a plan. A solid one," Leo states.

"But, with this plan, you two have to work together and not

argue because if you do then this will all go to shit," Cole says, looking between Alexander and me.

"Us?" I ask, looking at Alexander, but he looks just as confused as I am.

"Yes. You two are going to go to Russia."

"What?!" Alexander and I both say at the same time.

"The mole was going to go to Russia to meet up with one of the Russian soldiers who works at the estate with Vladimir and they were going to meet at this popular club that I now have the location of," my dad states holding up a piece of paper. "I want you two to go to that club and find out where the estate is located. After you find out the location, you will then fly back here, and we will continue to move forward with the plan."

"Plan?" I furrow my eyebrows.

"I will talk to you guys about that when you get back from the mission," my dad states. "One thing at a time."

"What do you want us to do?" Alexander asks.

"Like I said, I want you to go to Russia and talk to that guy about where the location is. Thalia, you will be doing most of the work and getting the information."

"Then why does Alexander need to come with me?" I raise my eyebrows.

"Do I really need to tell you that?" my dad says furrowing his eyebrows at me. "After tonight, you need someone with you at all times to make sure you don't do anything stupid. Especially since you are going to Russia, close to where the enemy is and he wants you both dead."

"Why not send someone else?"

"Because I don't trust them and plus since you want to go out and fuck around then you will get the chance to do that in Moscow."

"Do I have to go with him though?" I ask, pointing to Alexander. "I am pretty sure I can take care of myself."

Alexander chuckles. "As if."

I look at Alexander. "I'm sorry, who is the one who beat the other to a pulp during training the other day."

Alexander leans forward. "I was going easy, angel. Don't want to ruin the only good feature you have now, would I?"

"You're such a dick." I roll my eyes. "I can take care of myself and I certainly don't need you for anything. You are just a waste of a-"

"Cut it out!" my father yells. "I am so sick and tired of you two arguing nonstop. You argue over the stupidest shit," my dad rubs his temples and sighs. "You two need to get along because I am not going to go through this with the both of you every day because I swear to god you both have been nothing but dicks to each other since the start."

"You two need to learn how to get along and work together. Especially since you are going on this mission together," my mom says.

As I look at her, I notice how drained she looks. She has bags under her eyes, and I notice her jaw is more prominent, making me think she lost weight.

"You really do," Emma claims. "It's ridiculous that you guys always argue."

"It's not just me-"

"Stop," Leo says, cutting Alexander off.

I let out an annoyed sigh and look at Alexander who looks frustrated and is clenching his fist.

"Now, you both will be in Russia for the weekend. You and Alexander will go to the club and get that location. The next day you will get on a plane and come back here. I want you guys to be quick and get out of Russia as soon as you can."

"Anything else?" I ask in an annoyed tone.

"Pack your bags."

Thirteen

I GET OUT OF THE SHOWER AND WRAP A TOWEL AROUND my body at the same time I hear my phone ring.

I pick up the phone and put it to my ear as I walk back into the room. "Hello?" I ask, not knowing who it is.

I didn't look at the caller ID, so I had no clue who was calling.

"Hello, gorgeous," I hear Cameron say from the other side of the phone.

I feel my lips lift in a small smile. "Hey. What's up? I am kind of in a rush."

Alexander and I have a flight to get on to go to Russia soon and I want to take care of some last-minute things before heading out.

Like showering so I don't smell bad on the plane.

I did most of my packing yesterday which wasn't a lot because I just packed some clothes for when I go to sleep and then clothes for the mission. My dad also said he wanted Alexander and me to take a bag of weapons in case things get out of hand, which they won't.

"Oh, should I call you back? I just wanted to talk to you. I'm not doing anything, and everyone is out so I wanted to talk to you."

"No, we can talk. I'll just multitask," I chuckle.

"What are you doing right now?" he asks.

"Packing."

"For what?"

"I have a family trip I have to go on for a couple of days," I lie.

"Sounds fun. Where are you guys going?"

"America. My dad has a business meeting there, so he decided to take us along. It's been a while since we all had family time," I lie.

Except I will be with the dickwad himself.

I haven't seen him since the night my father told us that he wanted us to go on this mission, which was a day ago.

My dad also made sure to scold me for sneaking out, which I didn't because I literally walked out the front door where he could see me.

I argued with him and said that I am a twenty-year-old woman who is allowed to make her own decisions but of course he thought otherwise.

So, for now I am giving him the silent treatment because what he is doing isn't fair. I am pretty sure my father lived by himself when he was around my age and that he could do whatever the hell he wanted to.

When I did bring that point up to him, he just said that he was a man, and I am just a girl. Things are different than they were twenty years ago.

If my mom was around he probably would have said it in a different way though.

"That sounds fun."

"Yea. I am looking forward to it," I drop the towel from my body and put Cameron on speaker. "What about you? What are you doing?"

He starts talking but I'm not paying attention because I hear my bedroom door open and I see Alexander walk in.

"Hey, we have to go-" he stops talking only because his eyes widen and he's roaming them all over my body.

"Xander!" I yell and go to get the towel from the floor to cover my bare body but instead of Alexander moving he just leans on his side against the wall and smirks.

"Damn, De Luca, I didn't know you were kinky like that. Phone sex doesn't seem like your thing."

I feel heat rush to my cheeks, and I don't think twice before running towards him and shoving him out of the room.

"Fuck you!" I yell.

"You wish, angel," I hear him mutter, making me roll my eyes and kick the door.

Alexander saw me naked.

I shouldn't care but for some reason, I feel embarrassed, which is a first. Alexander has seen me in my underwear and bra before and I have never cared, but god, he saw me naked.

I feel embarrassed.

My cheeks feel like they are on fire and the spot between my legs aches.

"Thalia? Hello, are you still there?"

I run to the phone and take him off speaker before putting it to my ear. "Hey, sorry I need to go but I will text you."

"Is everything okay? I heard you yell and then someone else?" Cameron asks in a worried tone.

"Yeah, I'm fine, I need to go."

"Alright, bye," Cameron says at the same time I hang up the phone.

I quickly change into a pair of dark gray leggings and a shirt that is cropped. I quickly put on my shoes and run out of the room.

As I am running down the stairs, I see one of the maids wiping down the floor. "Meredith, can you please send someone to get my bags from my room?" I ask as I walk past her, and I see her nod her head. "Thank you."

I walk inside the kitchen and see the devil himself.

Alexander is sitting on a barstool next to my brother and they are just talking and laughing.

Alexander lifts his eyes so they meet mine and I see a challenging, amused glint in his eyes making me want to punch his face until he can't smirk or have that stupid amused smile on his face.

Killian turns his head and looks at me. "Hey, Thalia," Killian says with a smile still on his face.

I ignore him and walk towards Alexander so that I am standing right in front of him. "Is it hard to be a gentleman? Do you ever knock before walking into places?"

"If I knocked then I wouldn't have been blessed a few moments ago with what I saw, now would I?"

I give him a fake smile. "You're a pig. No wonder why girls wouldn't want a relationship with you."

"Angel, girls would die to have a relationship with me. It's me who doesn't want one with them."

"Why? Does their dick sucking need some work before they officially become yours?" I tease but then I feel Alexander pull me closer so that I am standing between his legs with his hand on my wrist.

"No, actually it's because none of them seem to meet my needs," he whispers harshly in my ear. "Why are you asking, Thalia? Jealous?"

I glare at him and push myself away from him. "As if I want to waste my time fucking you. I probably won't even feel satisfied afterwards," I spit and Alexander just glares at me.

"We can test it out and see?"

"Ew," Killian glares at the both of us. "Can you guys please not test out that theory in front of me?"

I look at Killian. "As if I want to test out that theory at all." I roll my eyes.

Alexander stands up from the stool and walks closer to me, up until he is so close to my face, our noses brush.

"You're such a little liar. Maybe if you admit it then maybe I won't edge you when we fuck. And trust me angel, I will fuck you, but it won't be because I make the first move, it will be because you're begging me to," Alexander whispers quietly so that Killian can't hear. I feel my heart rate picking up a little bit before Alexander moves past me. "We have to go."

I turn to look at Alexander, while also trying to show and convince myself that what he said didn't affect me.

My heart is racing quickly, and I wish it wouldn't.

"Where are we going?" I ask, my mind completely up in the sky, in scribbles, in the stars.

"Russia, angel."

Fourteen

"What the fuck do you mean that there is only one hotel room booked?" I ask the girl who works at the front desk of the hotel.

"I'm sorry miss but it says that there is only one room booked for both Xavier Volkov and Anastasia Alexei," the lady says in a thick Russian accent.

I sigh deeply. "Yeah well, I remember specifically ordering two rooms, not one, so either fix it or I will."

Right now, Alexander and I are trying to check into the hotel but they're saying we have to share a double bed hotel room and I want to be as far away from Alexander as possible.

"I'm sorry, but there is nothing I can do. Most of the rooms in this hotel are booked."

Before I can bring out my gun and shoot her head, I feel Alexander put his arm around my waist.

"It's fine. I'm sure that you have done everything you can,"

Alexander says with a small smile on his face. "We will be on our way."

The girl sent us a small smile before Alexander brought us inside the elevator. Luckily, there was no one in the elevator with us.

"Why the fuck did you do that?" I ask pushing him away from me.

"Do what?" Alexander deadpans.

"Not let me blow her brains out?"

Alexander looks at me. "Because if I did that, then that would ruin everything, and I don't want to stay in this goddamn country for long so sorry I kill-blocked you."

I roll my eyes and lean against the wall.

When the elevator door opens, Alexander and I walk to our room silently, not saying a word to each other. When we enter our hotel room, I see our bags placed on our beds. My bags were placed on the bed closer to the window in the room that is overlooking the city while Alexander's bags were placed on the bed that was next to mine.

Our other bag, which is filled with weapons, is next to the table that is right in front of the window.

I walk over to the window and see the city and some snow that is coming down. It is the middle of April, so I am shocked that there is light snow.

I feel my phone vibrate from inside my pocket making me take it out.

"Hello?"

"Hey baby, did you land okay?" my mother asks.

"Yea. Alexander and I are in the hotel room and Michael put

our bags and shit like that in our room."

Michael is basically my 'bodyguard' I guess you can say. My father made me bring one here and some other men because he wanted to make sure that there are no issues.

"Okay great. How was the flight?"

Fucking torture.

I couldn't sleep at all and when I finally did get a chance to sleep, we had already landed. Alexander was just working on the computer, and I couldn't help but watch him work for a little.

The way he furrowed his eyebrows and rubbed his forehead made me want to demand for him to get off the computer and go to sleep because he looked stressed out. He also looked kind of cute when he furrowed his eyebrows at something he didn't understand.

Ew, no, he didn't look cute what the fuck?

"Fine," I state.

"Did you guys take a look at the weapons?" my father says.

I didn't even know he was on the phone or near my mother.

"Not yet. But I know we have the mission tonight, so we were going to take a look at the plan and make sure everything is set," I say and look behind me only to see Alexander on the bed with his eyes closed.

I don't go over to wake him but something in my body is forcing me not to go over there and slap him until he is awake.

We also only have a few hours until we both have to get ready for the mission.

"I want to go over the plan one more time just to make sure you guys know what you're doing."

My father and his plans.

Every time there is a mission, he always makes sure to go over the plan five times before the actual mission.

"Well, Anastasia is going to be substituting one of the strippers at the club so I will go to the club all glammed up and Xavier will come minutes later all dressed up in a suit to protect little Anastasia in case anything happens to her," I deadpan.

Anastasia and Xavier are my and Alexander's names for while we are here in Russia because if anyone knew our real names then that will spread like wildfire, and we will get caught.

"Okay, and what will you do?"

I roll my eyes. "I will make sure to bring him in a room where it's just us two and I will get the location of the estate out of him and then I will kill him. Easy," I shrug.

"And then you will come back tomorrow morning so that we can move forward with the plan and be done with these fucking Russians."

"Sounds like a grand fucking plan dad."

"Don't fuck up, Thalia. I want you home in one piece. As well as Alexander, so try not to kill each other while you are there 'cause if you do, I will kill you and then ask Satan politely to bring you back to the world of the living and then make sure to give you a good, long lecture because I know how much you love lectures, Thalia."

I roll my eyes at my father's attempt to scare me. "Sounds fun dad. I'll text you before the mission. Love you," I say before hanging up the phone and throwing it on the bed.

Let's pray to god we both don't fuck up.

Fifteen

I walk inside the club and the song 'Woo' by Rihanna is playing on the speakers, loudly.

As I am walking through the club, I feel all eyes on me but I pay no mind to anyone.

I am wearing a black dress that has lacy fabric from the waist up and the dress goes down to my mid-thighs. It hugs my body in all the right areas. I am wearing a lacy underwear and bra set underneath the dress. My hair is also curled, and I have my makeup done lightly.

I never put on too much makeup but for these kinds of missions, I have to put makeup on and try a little harder than usual.

"My name is Anastasia Alexei. I am here to substitute Marie," I say to the guy who is in front of the dressing room for all of the girls.

"ID?" the guy asks.

I take my fake ID out of my wallet and give it to him. He looks through all of the information and hands it back to me.

Before we left for Russia, Alexander and I had to get fake IDs so that we could get inside the club and do what we need to do.

"All of the girls are in the back. You go up in fifteen minutes so hurry up and do whatever you need to do before you get on stage," the man states bluntly while looking down at the clipboard in his hand.

I don't say anything to him, I just pass him and go inside the room. Once I get inside the dressing room, I see all of the girls. They are all wearing their matching sets and have their hair and makeup done.

I can tell how much plastic surgery they have gotten as well because their boobs and asses look way too fucking big to be real and they are pushed up to their fucking chins. Their butts didn't look at all natural, but who am I to judge?

It's their body, they can do whatever the hell they want with it.

I mean, I have nipple piercings so again I can't judge because I have done shit to my body before that they would probably not approve of.

"Hey," a girl says.

I move my gaze to look at her. She has long, dark brown hair and bright blue eyes. She looks like a younger version of Megan Fox.

She is very beautiful, and she probably gets a lot of attention from the guys.

"Hi," I say, and showcase a bright smile to her. "I'm Anastasia."

"Yeah, I know. The girls and I were just talking about Marie's sub for tonight. I am Katrina."

"Nice to meet you." I give her a small smile. "So how do things work here?"

I know how they work. I am just trying to make conversation.

Katrina hooks her arm around my arm and pulls me more inside the room. "Well, basically all of the girls just get ready and change up until the stage manager calls us out for us to go on stage."

"Sounds easy."

She nods her head with a small smile on her face."So, are you ready 'cause I am pretty sure you are going up soon?"

"Yea I just need to take off my dress and find a place to put my stuff. Is there somewhere I can put it?"

"Yea, we have cubbies where you can put all of your things."

Katrina shows me where to put all of my belongings. She also introduces me to some of the girls and most of them look like models. They are all beautiful.

I change out of my dress and make sure my makeup is on point for when I go on stage.

"Anastasia Alexei. You're up." the stage manager says making me look at him instead of looking at the mirror.

"Good luck," Katrina says before I leave and I smile at her.

Once I walk on stage, I see everyone staring at me.

My eyes roam the crowd looking for Draco Babine, the person who I am supposed to kill tonight. My eyes go straight to Alexander who is sitting in one of the chairs up front with a girl on his lap. I saw her in the dressing room, she was one of those plastic bitches.

Of course, he would grab one of those girls, it's his type but he likes to deny it.

I resist the urge to roll my eyes and I continue walking forwards until I am front and center on the stage.

There is also a pole up front waiting for me.

I walk up to the pole and touch the metal bar before walking around it.

I feel so many eyes on me as I sway my hips while walking around the pole. When I face the audience again I make eye contact with Draco. His eyes roam up and down my body and he has a smirk on his face.

Dirty fucks.

I grab a hold of the pole and do a pirouette, which causes men to throw their money at me. I swing my body around the pole and then use my upper body strength to open my legs in a V-shape. I hear a lot of cheers once I do that.

I get off the pole and see Draco who has a smirk and my eyes trail down to his pants which have a tent.

Perfect.

He will want a private dance.

To make sure I lure him in more I walk off the stage towards him and sit in his lap. I place my lips directly next to his ear.

"So turned on and all because of little me?" I whisper while trailing my finger down his chest.

I feel him place a bill in my underwear and my eyes go up to Alexander who is sitting behind Draco.

That girl who was on his lap is now gone and he is only staring at me with a lustful look and furrowed eyebrows. His fists and jaw are clenched as he stares at me. I can see the small smirk teasing his lips as he starts to rub his thighs, slowly adjusting his pants.

I smirk at him and lick Draco's neck teasingly while still staring at Alexander.

I hear a lot of men yell and cheer for Draco, but I'm not paying any mind to them, I keep my gaze locked on Alexander.

'*Fuck you*' I mouth to him, and I see him smirk.

"Oh, I will, angel," I hear Alexander mumble, making the smirk on my face wipe off.

Sixteen

As I see Thalia walk out in a black lacy bra and thong, I shove the brunette who was sitting on my lap, away from me. My focus is purely on Thalia as she walks out, her heated eyes looking straight into mine as she walks up to the pole before walking around it, swaying her hips side to side.

She is finally facing forward again and my eye's gaze zones in on her boobs, more specifically her nipples. I can see the piercings behind the thin lacy material.

When I first saw her piercings the other day, when I walked in on her naked, I almost came in my pants like a teenager.

She is fucking breathtaking as she dances seductively.

Like a dark angel. My dark angel.

For a moment, she looks at only me as she dances, and I feel like it's just the two of us in the room. She is only dancing for me, walking closer until her hands touch my thighs, pushing them apart. She leans closer to me, and I stare at her as her breath feathers my lips. I want to lean forward and bite her lip until blood draws.

The sound of cheering makes me focus in on what's really happening, and I see Thalia sitting on Draco's lap, my hand starts squeezing the chair.

Thalia keeps her eyes trained on mine as she licks Draco's neck. All I want to do is shoot Draco's head and drag Thalia over my lap to show her she is mine.

Thalia mouths 'fuck you' to me and I can't help but smirk.

"Oh, I will, angel."

Thalia smirks and then presses a kiss to Draco's neck before getting off of him and walking back to the stage, leaving.

I didn't see Thalia and how she dressed or what she wore when she left. I was asleep while she was getting ready, and I woke up to an alarm and then a note from her saying to meet her at the club.

I thought we were going to go together but I guess not.

But shit, I didn't know I would get this hard from watching her spin on that fucking pole. Her black lingerie looked hot as fuck on her perfect tanned skin.

Shit.

I felt heat spread all throughout my body and then towards my cock making a tent grow in my pants, my bulge pressing against the zipper.

Then when she licked that fucking guy's neck, I wanted to kill him. I wanted to torture him and burn him alive while he prayed for mercy.

Little Thalia isn't so little anymore.

God, and when I saw her naked body the other day, I wanted to just shut the damn door and take her then and there but then I heard that kid, Cameron on the other side of the phone making me feel pissed off that she was talking to him, while naked as well.

I clench my fists tighter and stand up from the chair I was sitting on at the same time that shithead Draco stands up.

Draco is the guy we are supposed to kill tonight. Hopefully, when I kill him that will relieve some kind of tension in my body because right now, I am hard as shit, and I can't concentrate on anything.

I was hoping that girl on my lap would relieve me or suck me off but right when I saw Thalia walk on stage, that all went out the window. Now I only want her, and I intend to get that tonight or at least some part of her because I am fucking done with this shit.

I'm acting like a fucking horny ass twelve-year-old boy who just searched up on the internet how boobs looked.

And all because of Thalia fucking De Luca.

I walk to the bar which is also near the private rooms. I see Draco walking towards the guy in front of the hallway.

"Straight whiskey," I state to the bartender while staring at Draco and listening in on his conversation.

"I want to order a private dance."

Horny fucker.

But I mean who wouldn't be horny while staring at Thalia, I get a hard-on every day I am around her.

"With whom?" the man blocking the hallway says.

He is probably the room manager or something.

"The brunette on stage from just a few minutes ago. She was wearing black lingerie and her hair was curled."

"Anastasia Alexei?" the room manager says, and Draco nods his head. "Name?"

"Draco Babine."

He better not fucking touch her.

"Straight whiskey," the bartender says while giving me my drink.

I grab my drink while still listening to what they are saying.

"Alright, I will let her know. Wait a few minutes for me though, will you?" the floor manager says, and I hear Draco respond with a yes.

I downed the rest of my drink before turning around and walking to Draco. "Hey, man." I touch his shoulder. "There was a guy looking for you. He had really dark long hair and was wearing a suit I believe. The bartender told me to go to you and let you know," I say, explaining how Rasputin looks.

"Oh, shit. Thanks, dude. If the room manager comes, tell him I went to go check on something."

"For sure," I say before Draco leaves towards the bar.

Idiot.

I walk around the room manager's stand where he probably keeps all of the files about the rules and where whose room is at.

I see a binder labeled 'Girl's Rooms' so I take it and open it to where Anastasia's name is at. I see her name next to the girl she is substituting so I close the book and walk down the hallway where the rooms are.

I see Anastasia's room number, so I open the door and see no one inside.

Good.

There are pink LEDs all over the room and then a long couch against the wall. There is also a small stage with a pole front and center and a small bar to the side where they hold the drinks.

I hear footsteps coming forwards making me hide behind the curtain that is near the stage.

I hear the door open, and I peek and see it is Thalia wearing her lacy bra and underwear reminding me of how hard I was while watching her on stage.

Shit.

Thalia closes the door behind her and walks fully inside the room looking around. I walk out front from behind the curtain, and she has her back turned to me, letting me see a nice view of her round ass.

Shit, I need to fuck her right now.

I will.

On every fucking piece of furniture that's around me.

I walk towards her and before she can turn around and cut my face with the knife she has hidden in her underwear, I grab her arms and pull her against me with her back against my chest, making me feel her ass right against my cock. "Fucking naughty," I whisper in her ear. "I thought I was supposed to do the dirty work and kill him," I whisper while trailing my lips along her neck.

"Stop messing around Alexander. Draco is going to be here any minute," Thalia whispers back but she doesn't move from my hold.

"He is busy looking for someone who is dead, angel," I whisper before pressing my lips to the nape of her neck. "You know how horny you made people out there?" I slide my hands to her hips and play with the lace fabric.

"Alexander," Thalia says in a breathy tone.

I run my hands down towards where her pussy is. "Tell me to stop, Thalia."

"You couldn't find a whore in the crowd to satisfy your needs?" Thalia says while trying not to moan as I cup her between her thighs.

"Didn't tell me to stop yet, Thalia," I say in her ear before nipping at the lobe. Thalia lets out a small moan and rests her head on my shoulder. "Mmm?" I say while looking down at her.

God, I like this sight. Seeing her trembling against me.

Before she can answer, I hear voices and footsteps outside of the room. I completely let go of Thalia and hide behind the curtain that I was hiding behind before she walked into the room.

I hear the door open, and footsteps walk in.

"Are you alright?" I hear Draco ask, making me peek out of the curtain to see what's going on.

Seventeen

I shake my hands that were by my sides, getting the nerves I was feeling out. I turn and look at Draco.

I give him a small smile. "Of course. I'm fine, just nervous."

And fucking horny now.

The cold blade I hid under my lace underwear was making me shiver and feel aroused. Alexander fucking around with me wasn't helping.

"Don't be nervous, sweetheart. You're absolutely breathtaking," Draco says before walking towards me.

"Thank you," I say shyly.

Draco smiles at me and walks behind me to go sit on the long couch in the back of the room.

Here we go.

God why did Alexander have to do that, especially right now, out of all fucking times.

I walk towards Draco and straddle his lap. I put my hands on his shoulders and lean down to touch his ear with my lips.

"You want me?" Draco whispers and I try not to roll my eyes.

I press a small kiss below his ear. "Yea, but I also want something else."

I feel Draco place his hands on my ass and he also encourages me to move my hips against his. I also feel his growing erection pressing into me.

"Oh, yea? What do you want sweetheart? Tell me."

I lean closer to his ear. "I want to know where the estate of Vladimir Ivanov is," I whisper sensually.

Draco backs away from me and I see him furrow his eyebrows. "What?"

I raise my eyebrow and slide my hands down his biceps. "You heard me handsome."

"I have no clue what you are talking about," Draco says while trying to hide his shocked expression.

Draco tries to get me off, but I grab his arms and hold them against the wall above his head.

I lean down and kiss his neck. "Come on. I'll give you a reward," I say, in a sensual tone.

"I-I uh-"

He gets cut off when I get pulled off of his lap by Alexander.

I land on the floor while Alexander holds Draco to the wall. "Fucking tell me where Vladimir Ivanov's estate is and maybe I won't kill you slowly," Alexander threatens.

Draco raises his eyebrows and looks between Alexander and me. "Holy shit, you're them."

I stand up from the floor and walk behind Alexander who is still holding Draco against the wall.

"I'm surprised you just found that out now," I state and put my hand on Alexander's shoulder.

God, he feels so tense.

"Tell me where the estate is now," Alexander demands.

"He isn't even scared. All you are doing is holding him against the wall," I sneer at Alexander, and he just grunts in response.

Asshole.

I get the knife I hid under my underwear and pull it out to hold it against Draco's neck. "Now, Alexander here doesn't know how to properly kill someone so I can use you for an example if you don't tell us where it is," I say in a threatening tone. Draco isn't answering, he is just looking between Alexander and me. I press the knife against his neck, and I see blood dripping down and Draco wincing. "Tell me now or I will just stab you until you tell me."

"Fuck you, you she-devil."

"Nah, she is no devil. Only the worst angel I know but no devil," Alexander says with a smirk.

"Can you stop with that fucking nickname? It's so stupid," I say to Alexander.

Alexander looks at me and I see a small, amused smirk on his face still. "Never, angel."

"Okay I am done with this bullshit," I shove Alexander away from Draco so that I can hold him against the wall. "If you don't tell me the location, I will poke your eye out with this blade," I say while trailing the knife along his jaw. "So, tell me. I am not going to ask again."

Draco doesn't say anything, so I take my knife and hold it close in front of his eye. I move my knife right under his eye and I dig the blade into his skin making him cry.

"Shit, okay okay," Draco says, making me stop and stare at him. "Malaya Bronnaya St, 65, Moscow, Russia 122221. Only twenty minutes away from here," Draco says while shutting his eyes.

I look back at Alexander. "Look it up," I look back at Draco. "If you are lying, I would start praying."

After a few seconds Alexander finds the location. "He's right. Now let me kill him," Alexander shuts his phone and walks up from behind me.

I look back at Draco. "You know I still haven't figured out what to say before I kill someone. My father usually says to save a seat for him next to Satan or to say hi to Satan for him. I think it's kind of cheesy and I am still trying to figure out what to say," I say while trailing my knife near his eye. "But I think I am just going to keep it simple," I lean closer to his ear. "*Ci vediamo all'inferno.*"

I then stab him in the eye before walking away from him. Draco screams in pain and tries to walk towards me but Alexander holds him against the wall.

"I am going to enjoy killing you," Alexander says while giving Draco a sadistic smile. "You touched something that was mine to touch. So instead of a quick, easy death. I am going to make sure you suffer."

Although I feel like rolling my eyes to his words, the way he said them did make me want to rub my thighs together as I feel heat between my legs.

Alexander grabs the knife out of his eye and then stabs his neck, where his vocals cords are located.

Guessing he did that so that Draco wouldn't make much noise.

Alexander took the knife out of his neck and then flipped it in his hand.

"Prick," Draco says in a raspy voice but I can tell it hurt him to say that.

"Yea I have been called that way too many times to not even care," Alexander shrugs before taking the knife and stabbing it in his shoulder and dragging the knife down his arm. Draco winces and tries to yell but nothing comes out of his mouth. "Okay, if you tell me to stop then I will. Just let me know," Alexander says before taking the knife out and stabbing his other shoulder and bringing the knife down.

Draco yells and tries to tell Alexander to stop but nothing comes out of his mouth.

Shame.

"Can we hurry up? If you don't just kill him then we will get caught," I deadpan.

"Shut the fuck up," Alexander says before bringing the knife out of Draco's body and stabbing his chest. "*Addio, figlio di puttana,*" Alexander sneers before dragging the knife down and making Draco's eyes fall.

Blood is dripping down his body and Alexander has some blood on his suit as well.

Alexander lets go of Draco making him fall limp to the floor. Alexander turns around and I feel like I am going to faint.

Okay, a little dramatic but, damn.

Alexander's white suit has blood stains on it. His hair is messy as well and he has some blood splattered on his neck and face.

Some girls would find this sight traumatizing and scary but me?

I find this one hell of a sight. I want to take him right now because ever since I got on stage and he was watching me with that lustful look I felt bothered and hot.

I don't know if it's because I haven't had sex in a while but I want to have Alexander fuck me, but I would never admit that out loud.

"Shit," I say, not knowing what else to say.

"Let's go," Alexander says before taking my hand and leading us out the door.

"Wait, I need my dress."

"Angel, by the end of the night that dress will be shredded to pieces," Alexander says looking back at me.

I let out a breath I didn't even know I was holding. "I am not walking outside where it's freezing cold, in underwear and a bra," I deadpan.

Alexander sighs deeply. "Thalia, I hope you are going to be ready for what I have planned when we get to that hotel room because there is no way in hell I am letting you go anywhere after."

"We'll see," I smirk before walking past him out of the private room.

Alexander Russo is going to be the death of me.

Eighteen

Once Thalia is done changing, I drag her out of the club and bring her into my car that is parked right out front.

I don't care if she brought a car with her or not, as long as we get to the hotel before my balls fucking explode.

"What's got you all tense?" Thalia asks in a teasing tone as I drive through the streets.

"You love to play games with me, angel, but let's see how well you do playing my kind of games because I am positive that you won't survive," I say while staring straight at the road.

Thalia then laughs.

She fucking laughs and I grip the wheel tighter and grunt in response.

"I'd love to see the type of games you play, Alexander. Tell me is it anything like the games you play with your little whores?"

I look at Thalia and see her raising her eyebrows with an amused smile.

"Oh, baby, never. With you, it will always be the best kind of game, but you see this little game we have been playing has been going on for too long now and I think I have had enough."

"What game?" Thalia asks in an innocent tone as she turns in her seat, so she is facing me, and lays her feet on my lap.

I feel my cock get harder as I keep driving. "Oh, angel I think you know the kind of game and it has been going on for too fucking long."

The rest of the drive to the hotel is silent. The tension between us is growing and I can't fucking take it.

I park the car and get out, going to Thalia's side of the car and pulling her out as well. I pull her next to me as we walk inside the hotel. I ignore all of the looks people give us.

I mean, why wouldn't they look at us. We look like a train wreck.

Thalia is wearing a skimpy ass outfit and I have blood stains on my white dress shirt while holding my blood-stained white suit coat.

When we get inside the elevator, I push her against the wall and once the doors of the elevator close I look down at her.

"Ready to have this game over with?" I ask with a raised eyebrow. Thalia doesn't answer me, so I lean down, my lips brush against hers. I feel her shiver under me, making me smirk down at her. "You nervous, angel?"

"Around you? Never," Thalia smirks while staring at me with those gorgeous sparkly green eyes.

That's it.

I can't take it.

I need her.

I need to taste her.

So, I do.

I lean down and crash my lips on hers.

I am not going to lie, I thought she was going to push me away and slap me in the face but instead she squirms against me, freezes, and then lets out a moan.

God, she tastes better than I imagined.

She tastes like fucking vanilla. She always wears vanilla perfume and every time she passes me, I feel like I am going to faint. Vanilla is her signature scent. She literally lathers herself in vanilla shampoo and body wash and the lip balm she is wearing tastes like fucking vanilla.

God, I want to devour her.

Her fingers curl into my shirt and my little angel does the last thing I expect, she kisses me back while melting into me. My hand wraps around the base of her skull and she trembles against me. Our sins wash away in this euphoric rush. We are both desperate and hungry for more. And for a second, I can't even remember why she is my enemy.

My tongue slips into her mouth and she moans.

But that soon washes away when I hear the bell ring making her pull away from me and turn her head to see who the hell interrupted this amazing fucking moment.

I see an older woman.

She is looking between Thalia and me with a shocked expression while also smirking at us. Thalia groans and rests her head on my shoulder while I have an amused smile on my face. I pick her up, making her wrap her legs around my waist instantly. And before she can argue with me, I press my mouth on her and slip my tongue into her mouth.

I walk out of the elevator and bring her over to our hotel room door. I hold her against the hotel room door and dig into my pocket looking for the hotel key card while still kissing her but when I can't find it, I groan and remove my lips from Thalia.

"Fuck," I look down and still hold Thalia against the wall as she kisses down my neck.

I feel more heat rush to my cock as she presses her lips to my neck.

Once I finally find the key, I press it to the door and open it so that Thalia and I can fucking get in.

I open the door and then slam it shut before dropping Thalia to the floor and pushing her against the door.

I put my lips back on hers and then trail them down her neck. "Xander," she says my name while clenching her thighs together.

"Stop fucking saying my name like that and clenching your thighs together unless you want me to give you a reason to keep them apart," I mutter against her skin. Normally the nickname makes me mad but right now, it's all I want to hear. I like the way she says it while I kiss her soft skin. Thalia whimpers against me. I take my hand and trail it up her thigh where I feel heat radiating from her cunt. When I move the fabric to the side, I can feel how wet she is. "Definitely wetter than I thought," I say in her ear before giving it a gentle bite to the lobe and then picking her up by her legs. "All because of me too."

I walk over to the bed while kissing her and then I drop her on the mattress. "Xander, please," Thalia begs.

I put my hands on her waist and trail them down her thighs, touching her soft silky skin.

"What do you want, angel?" I ask before kneeling in front of her, my thigh pressed against her cunt.

She grinds her hips down and her eyes flutter closed.

I pull my thigh away and grab her underwear and push them to the side, bringing my thumb up to suck on it before bringing it down to rub slow eight figures on her clit.

"You," she gasps.

"Got to be more specific, angel."

I decide to tease her a little bit and dip my finger into her aching hole before bringing it out.

"God, you Xander. Your mouth, your fingers, your . . .your fucking cock," she cries. "If you make me beg again then I will order another goddamn room and just fuck myself."

I look up at her and raise my eyebrows. "Really? Are you sure?"

Thalia squirms and tries to lift her hips closer to my face, but I push them down to the bed. "Please, Xander. If you want me to beg, then fine I am begging you, just do something."

"All you had to do was that, angel," I say before leaning down and diving into her, kissing her like it was her lips.

God, tastes just like fucking vanilla. Somehow someway she tastes so fucking sweet.

Since the cloth is in the way, I rip it off and throw it somewhere behind me. Thalia gasps and brings her hands down to my hair. I hook my arms around her thighs, and she spreads them a little wider, grinding up towards my face.

"God."

I swirl my tongue around while staring up at her, seeing her breathing heavily. I purse my lips around her clit and latch on to it before letting it go slowly.

"You have no idea how badly I have been wanting to taste this pretty little pussy of yours."

I keep repeating what I am doing but making sure she will eventually cum and when she finally does, it feels like barely a minute.

"God," she moans.

I watch her shake and feel her grip my hair as I fuck her gently with my tongue. My eyes roll to the back of my head as I lick all of her juices up.

"That's a good girl," I say standing up and taking off my dress shirt. I pull her closer to me by her thighs. I take off her dress and throw it behind me. I look down at her body and almost drool from the sight. "God, you are so fucking beautiful." I lean down and kiss her while lifting her upper body to take off her bra. When I take it off I back away and look down at her breasts that are most definitely pierced. "When did you get these?" I say while touching the metal that is pierced through her nipple.

Thalia squirms and starts to rub her thighs together. "A few weeks ago."

"Jesus," I bring my face down and kiss her breasts while also flicking the other nipple and playing with the piercing.

I lean away from her, remembering the massive boner I fucking have.

I need to be inside her.

Now.

I lean away from her and spread her thighs as far as I can. I bring my pants down, along with my briefs. I see my tip almost leaking at the sight in front of me.

Never thought I would see the day Thalia fucking De Luca was in front of me on a bed with her legs wide open and her hair all fucked up.

I lean down on her and cover her body with mine. Once my tip reaches inside her I groan and hide my face in the nape of her neck. Thalia moans as I move all the way inside her slowly. Those fucking sounds she was making as she took me.

Once our hips meet she gasps and her eyes slowly open and I can tell she wants to smile from how good it feels.

I look down as I pull out and see her coating me.

My eyes flutter closed as I move back inside her.

Fuck.

I keep a steady pace for a little even though I want to go rougher and faster but seeing her squirming and wanting more just brings me so much pleasure.

"God, Xander just fuck me already."

She grinds into me and I start going faster.

"Fucking naughty girl. Dancing on a pole and flirting with those boys and shit," I grunt and fuck her harder. Her eyes roll back so much she probably sees nothing but darkness. My breathing was rough, and I bet my hair was a mess from how many times I ran my fingers through it. I bring my hands down to spread her ass cheeks apart to give me more room. "Talk shit now, Thalia."

"Oh, my-oh my god, fuck!" she screams making me know that I found her fucking spot.

I fuck her harder and faster before she cums around me making me follow right after, shooting my load inside her.

She is going to be the fucking death of me.

Nineteen

I hear a beeping sound, waking me up from unconsciousness.

I open my eyes and turn to the side table and press the off button on my phone making the beeping stop.

I hear a groan next to me making me turn around and see Alexander with his eyes closed. His hair is a mess and that's probably because of how much he was moving in the bed.

I look down at his puffy, parted lips and see his tattooed chest heaving up and down.

God, he looks good.

He always looks good.

I look around the room and see that it is a mess. Some stuff that was on counters is now on the floor.

Alexander wasn't kidding when he said he would fuck me on every piece of furniture.

The events of last night came rolling in and it hit me like a fucking truck of how Alexander fucked me.

The heat in my stomach makes me want to reach inside and take it out.

Alexander and I had sex and although it was probably the most pleasurable experience ever, it feels wrong. I thought I hated him but last night was far from hate. Or maybe he and I fucked because we hate each other so much. It's all so confusing.

But no matter what it can never happen again. Alexander is nothing but a fuckboy who doesn't care about other people's feelings while I am just a girl who was horny and needed a way to feel satisfied and after last night I have never felt so satisfied in my life.

His touch on my skin felt like fire and I loved how he felt inside me and when he kissed me everywhere. Every time he kissed me, I felt shivers going down my body and then fireworks exploding in my stomach.

But it can't happen again.

It never will.

I look down at Alexander and see his eyes are still closed while one of his arms is behind his head, making his biceps look bigger than usual.

Jesus.

If any part of a man's body makes me weak it's his biceps and back muscles. It's just a hot feature that guys have.

I get out of the bed slowly and walk over to my suitcase that is in the closet. I grab out a change of clothes and quickly change into them before grabbing my suitcase and walking out of the hotel room.

Surely Alexander will understand, I mean he literally does this for a living. After he is done fucking girls, he either sends them to fuck off or he leaves before they can wake up.

I just don't want to be in the same room with him when he wakes up and ends up being an asshole again. I can deal with him when we get home or when he gets home because I am not staying in this damn country any longer. I just want to get home and relax. Besides, I don't do one-night stands and I know that with Alexander this is what this is. I have only had sex with two people in my life, now three.

God, I am now like one of those other girls who had sex with him. He probably sees me as a whore especially with the outfit I was wearing yesterday.

I get outside of the hotel and see the car I had ordered parked in the front.

I get inside the car. "The airport," I say and relax in the seat.

"What about Mr. Russo, Ms. De Luca?" the driver asks.

"He is taking his own plane."

After I say that, he knows not to question anymore so he starts driving to the airport while I look outside and watch the buildings pass by.

It isn't really snowing today or raining. You can see the dark gray clouds in the sky though. Although we are at war with Russia, the country itself is beautiful. I have only been to Moscow a few times and then I also went to Saint Petersburg once for a mission, but I also got to see the Romanov's castle because I watched the movie Anastasia and it's my favorite movie. The castle is beautiful and I am glad I got to see it in person.

"Ms., we are here," the driver says and I look up and see we are in front of the plane at the airport.

"Thank you. Do you mind getting my bags and putting them on the plane?" I ask as I unbuckle my seatbelt.

"Not at all, Ms.," he says before getting out of the car and going to the trunk to get my bag.

I get out of the car and put my phone in my pocket after texting my mom and dad telling them I am getting on the plane.

I close the car door and walk towards the stairs that lead up to the entrance of the plane but before I can place my foot in front of the other, I feel something shoot into my neck making me wince and turn around to see what the fuck is going on but when I do, I see a brown fabric being put over my head and then I let the darkness take over, making me fall limp and feel nothing.

Twenty

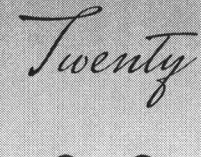

The sounds of knocking on the door wake me up and I groan in response but don't open my eyes.

"Sir, we must go, the plane is going to be departing soon." I hear Michael say from the other side of the door.

Fuck.

Already?

"What time is it?" I yell but still keep my eyes closed.

I shouldn't yell because Thalia is probably sleeping next to me.

"It's the afternoon sir. I will be waiting downstairs with the car."

I groan one more time before opening my eyes and turning to the side only to see no Thalia. Instead, I see the place where she slept is empty.

The fuck?

I look around the room and see that it is a mess, but I couldn't care less.

I get out of the bed and grab my briefs from the floor and slip them on. I walk through the hotel room and see that Thalia isn't here and neither are her bags.

She fucking left.

Fucking Thalia.

I go back to bed and grab my phone. I look through my contacts before finding her contact. I press it and put the phone to my ear. After the phone rings over and over, I hear her voicemail making me end the call and call her back.

I did that five more times and she still didn't answer.

The fuck.

I call one more time and wait for Thalia's voicemail.

"Hey, this is Thalia's voicemail. Sorry I couldn't get back to you but if you leave a voice message then I will be sure to get back to you but if I don't just text me. Bye!"

"Thalia, answer the fucking phone right now. If you don't then next time I fuck you I will make sure to edge you and not let you cum so answer me." I threaten after her voicemail greeting ends.

I also open the messages app and text her.

'Answer the fucking phone, Thalia'

'I'm not going to ask again if you don't answer I swear to Satan himself I will make sure the next time I call you, you will come to me on your knees waiting for me'

'Thalia if you think I am playing around you are dead wrong, answer the fucking phone'

I throw my phone on the bed and walk inside the closet to get my change of clothes which is just a pair of gray sweatpants and a black shirt. I don't bother cleaning the room because the hotel will take care of that. Instead, I get my shit and get out of the door while still calling Thalia's phone.

How the fuck did she get out of the room without waking me up?

Better question, why the fuck did she leave without me?

She really pulled that one-night stand bullshit where you leave before the other person wakes up.

But why?

Did she not like how we fucked last night?

Did I do something wrong?

The only questions in my head right now are why the fuck did she leave and then where the fuck is she.

I thought she wasn't stupid enough to leave the country without me, but I guess she is.

Who the fuck did she leave with if Michael is with me though? Did she leave with Peter or something?

I get outside and it's freezing balls out here. I see the car in the front with Michael in the driver's seat.

I get inside the car and put my bag on the seat next to me. "Do you know where Thalia is, Michael?"

"I believe she left with Peter in the other plane. She requested to take a separate plane," Michael states as he drives onto the street.

"Do you know why?"

The fuck am I doing?

Asking about her as if she is my girlfriend.

I mean she is mine and everyone should know that. After last night she is most certainly mine.

Honestly, I thought after one round I would get over her and not care for her anymore but then I found myself deep inside her over and over and over again.

I liked it.

A whole fucking lot and I want to do it again. I fucking need to do it again with her.

All of the other girls are now immediately thrown out the window. I only want her. I have always wanted her but after last night I am fucking certain. It wasn't just a hate fuck with her. She probably sees it like that though, knowing her. I doubt she admits her real feelings to herself though.

Fucking Thalia.

Still after years of trying to hate her I'm still obsessed with her.

"She didn't say, and Peter texted me that they left an hour ago," Michael states and I see him with an amused smile on his lips, looking at me through the rearview mirror. "Why, Russo?"

I smirk at him. "Fuck off."

Michael and I have grown pretty close over the years. I see him as a big brother. Although he is a bodyguard, I rarely treat him like one. I would call him my best friend out of everyone I talk to.

All of my friends usually want me for power or money, and I am not into that shit. Before I graduated, I dropped all of my friends in high school. I didn't feel like keeping them. They are all going to college to live a happy, safe life while I go on missions killing people, risking myself every day to fucking make sure that our empire doesn't fall while also hating and lusting after a girl who doesn't give two fucks about me, I bet.

But after last night I am starting to believe otherwise.

Just the way she said my name, the name I hate, Xander.

Usually, I hate that name and I hate when she calls me that but now every time she calls me that I am probably going to go back to last night and imagine her moaning my name while also scratching my back, marking me.

"Why did she leave?" Michael asks.

"'Cause she is scared. No matter how badass people make her out to be, in reality, she is a scared little girl who is secretly an angel afraid to admit her true feelings," I deadpan.

And if she doesn't then I won't give her what she wants.

"How do you know?"

"Because Thalia is the one person I know the most without even trying to know her. I know what she wants but she is afraid. She doesn't want to be vulnerable, especially with me for some weird reason that I don't know about."

Whatever.

Fuck her.

"Ever thought that Thalia might hate you instead of pretending to not admit her feelings?"

"No. Thalia doesn't hate me because she has no reason to hate me. I hated her because of some stupid childish thing when I was six but last night things felt different."

And instead of just staying and talking it out with me she left like a scared little bitch.

I clench my fists and look out the window.

"Getting soft, Russo?"

I chuckle. "For Thalia De Luca? Always."

I mean the girl makes me go crazy. Even when she isn't around me, I feel fucking insane.

Twenty One

I look through the messages between Thalia and me and I see that she still hasn't answered.

After almost four fucking hours she still hasn't answered.

God, I sound like I am obsessed with her and maybe I am but, seriously?

During the whole entire flight, I have been sleeping and waking back up constantly. I hate flights. I can never go to fucking sleep and when I do, I always wake back up for some reason.

Michael is sitting in one of the chairs playing on his phone. For the first hour of the flight, I was still trying to get a hold of Thalia but no luck, so I just gave up.

But she is going to have to face me soon, whether she likes it or not.

Once the plane lands I look out the window and see that we are, in fact, back home.

Thank fucking god.

I look at Michael. "Do you know if Thalia's plane landed?" I ask Michael while standing up from my seat and walking towards the exit of the plane.

"No. But Mr. De Luca texted me asking me where she went."

I furrow my eyebrows. "Shouldn't she be home already?"

"Yea that's what I don't understand. I texted him back, but he just left me on read."

"Maybe she is at home then," I shrug.

Michael and I get off of the plane and he gets my bags while I get inside the car.

The drive home isn't that long. Michael is driving me to the De Luca estate because Ace wants to have a meeting. He texted me saying that he wants to talk about the mission and something else, but he didn't tell me.

Honestly, my mind isn't on that though. It is still on the fact that fucking Thalia didn't answer any of my calls or texts and she left without me. I am so pissed off. At first, I was just confused but now I am mad and frustrated.

Once we get to the estate, Michael parks the car in the driveway and I get out and go inside the house. I walk through the house and it's empty, so I go to where Ace's office is. I knock on his door once I am in front of it and wait for him to give me the go ahead to go inside.

Ace doesn't let anyone go inside his office without knocking, only Thalia, Killian, and Aria.

"Come in," I hear Ace say, making me open the door and walk inside.

I see Aria sitting on Ace's lap with tears in her eyes as Ace rubs her lower back and looks at her with love and sympathy in his eyes.

My mom and dad are sitting on the couch with sad expressions on their faces.

What the fuck?

Ace turns his head to look at me and his facial expression changes. His fists are clenched and he looks mad as shit. He looks like he is going to punch something, anything.

Maybe me.

"What's wrong?"

"Sit," Ace states and I refrain from rolling my eyes and walk to the chair in front of his desk and sit down. "What the fuck happened while you and Thalia were in Russia?"

Where the fuck is Thalia?

That's my question.

"Nothing," I shrug. "We took care of Draco and I killed him after getting the location of the Ivanov's estate," I say, while digging in my pocket and getting the location of the estate and giving it to Ace. "Where's Thalia?"

"That's what I am trying to figure out, Alexander. You see, my daughter left Moscow before you yet you are here before her? I have been trying to call Peter, but he hasn't been answering."

"So, what the fuck? What's wrong?" I furrow my eyebrows.

"We think that Vladimir got her. Peter isn't answering his phone, neither is Thalia and I am wondering why the fuck my daughter and you didn't go on the same fucking plane together? I thought I told you guys to come here together?"

I clench my fist at the thought of Thalia being somewhere else other than here.

Is she with the Russians?

Or did she really run away because she didn't want to face me?

Was she that afraid?

God, I don't fucking know what to do.

"I thought so too, Ace, but your daughter likes being a bitch to me for no reason," I spit without even thinking.

Ace will probably punch me but I couldn't care less.

I am pissed and will probably need a good distraction after this shit.

"Watch it. Just because you are Leo's son doesn't mean I will not punch you. Watch how you talk about my daughter," Ace threatens and I roll my eyes.

"Your daughter is the one who left without me and decided to do things on her own. I was sleeping when she left, and she didn't bother to wake me up. Instead, she left."

Like a scared little bitch.

"Why did she leave though, Alexander? She had no reason to leave unless you pissed her off so what the fuck did you do?!" Ace yells, getting frustrated.

"Ace, calm down. We don't even know if Thalia was kidnapped or not," Aria says, trying to calm him down.

Ace looks at Aria. "Aria, what do you think she did? Went on some fucking vacation with fucking Peter? I don't think so," Ace chuckles darkly before turning his attention to me. "What happened, Alexander?"

I lightly shake my head and lean towards him. "I didn't do shit, Ace. Maybe when your daughter comes you can ask her yourself but until then, leave me alone. I got what you needed, therefore, you don't need me anymore."

I stand up from my chair and walk out of his office while Ace calls after me.

I don't give a shit though.

I need something.

A distraction.

A good one.

I could go to the gym and take my anger out by punching the bag or I can get high as shit or wasted.

Seems like the best option.

I get inside the car where Michael is still sitting in the driver's seat.

"Take me to my place," I state, and Michael doesn't say anything else, he just drives without replying. He probably knows I am not in the mood for bullshit. While he drives, I lean my head on the head rest and close my eyes. I feel the car park and I lift my head and see we're at my place. "Thanks," I say before getting out of the car and walking to the front door.

When I walk in, all of my lights are off. I go to the gym that is in the backyard. I take off my shirt and grab a blunt before lighting it and taking hits.

Once I finish smoking the blunt, I wrap my hands and go towards the punching bag.

I send punches to the bag as my mind races with possibilities and everything that is Thalia De Luca.

Twenty Two

FUCKING CUNTS.

They can't keep me in here forever.

It's been three days since they kidnapped me. Peter is fucking dead, they killed him.

Russians are assholes. They haven't fed me any food at all. They better fucking feed me a five-course meal because I swear if my stomach growls one more time then I will probably just take one of the guard's guns and shoot them in the head like I did with the others.

That's why Vladimir chained me to the wall.

I still haven't even gotten the chance to meet him. He has only been sending guards in the room, making sure I wasn't going to escape.

After Vladimir's men kidnapped me, I woke up in this dark room on the floor with a bruise on my neck from how they drugged me. I felt so dizzy and like I was going to go back to sleep or faint again.

Then, when I killed one of their men, they started to beat me and then they chained me to the wall.

They can't chain me to the wall forever.

Idiots.

I hear the door open making me look up and see a bright light making me squint my eyes. I see a guy's silhouette walking closer to me before the door closes. I try to get my eyes used to the darkness once again and once I do I see a man with dark brown hair and blue eyes.

I look back down at the ground instead of looking up at the guy. "You can tell your boss I am not dead yet." I then feel someone's hands on my chin forcing me to look up. "Get your hands off of me before I cut them off!"

"With what, *printsessa*?" the guy says in a harsh tone while trailing his eyes all over my face.

"I'm not going to ask again," I deadpan.

"Shame," the guy says before leaning closer to me. "Name is Vladimir Ivanov," he whispers and then leans away to see my reaction.

I keep a straight face and still stare at him.

So this is the famous Vladimir Ivanov?

He looks much older than I thought he would be. He looks like he is in his late twenties. I thought he would be Alexander and I's age, but I guess not.

He doesn't look ugly for a Russian but he has soft features and I like guys who aren't Russian and have stronger, mature faces.

I put a weak smirk on my face. "Vladimir Ivanov." I chuckle lightly. "You are the all-mighty Vladimir Ivanov? Thought you would be more-" I trail my eyes down his figure, "more." I shrug and then I feel a harsh slap on my face.

Jackass.

I am going to kill him. Not a quick death because that's too easy.

If he had any family, maybe a daughter or son or wife, I would kill them in front of him slowly and painfully and then I would kill him. I would skin his entire body and then light him up like a fucking firework before blowing up this shitty estate.

"You have balls," Vladimir chuckles.

I laugh like a fucking maniac. "You are going to wish you never kidnapped me 'cause I swear to god, when I get out of these chains, I am going to kill your family and then you and then every other shitty person in this hell hole," I threaten. "I'm going to *make you wish you were dead.*"

"I can't wait, but for now, I am going to have a little fun with you," Vladimir chuckles and he lets go of my face and walks a few feet away from me before staring down at me again.

Bet he liked what he was seeing.

Me, with sweat on my face and my arms chained to the wall, looking helpless and destroyed.

"So, what does little Ivanov want from little De Luca? Are you trying to finish what your father started?"

"No. I want to do something my father wasn't capable of. You see, my father was stupid with everything he was doing, but me? I have a plan set. I know what I am doing."

"What is so different from you and your father?"

"I will succeed while he watches me from hell. I will sleep soundly in my bed knowing that I am satisfied with what I have done to make all of you fucking Italians and Americans pay for what you have done."

I raise my eyebrow. "What did we do, Ivanov? Take away your gorgeous palace and burn it to the ground along with the only people who might have cared about you?"

I can tell what I said made him mad, so he walks closer to me and grabs a hold of my neck, pushing it against the wall.

"I would be careful if I were you," he whispers in my ear. "I am the one who decides whether you should stay alive or not. I can kill you right now."

"Then do it," I smirk.

Vladimir chuckles. "Not yet. I first need you for something but don't worry, I will make sure to have fun with you before you die. But not the fun you think."

"Sounds terrific. Can't wait," I tease. "Should I save the date on my calendar?" I say with sarcasm.

Vladimir clenches his jaw and then punches me in the face. "You are going to wish you never came to this goddamn country," Vladimir then turns around and walks towards the door.

He leaves the room while I spit out blood.

Fucker threw a punch towards my lip making my teeth dig into the skin.

I lean my head against the stone wall and close my eyes.

God, I wish this would be over.

I was just trying to get home and not have to deal with

Alexander but now I totally regret doing that. I wish he was with me, protecting me or telling me it was going to be okay.

I just want to go home but I need to be strong. I need to put up a strong front.

Twenty Three

I roll over on my bed and check my phone, seeing a message from Ace telling me to go to his office for a meeting.

It's been three days since I got back from Moscow and Thalia still hasn't been found yet. Aria has been worried sick while I have been alone in my house.

Ace keeps threatening me to get to his estate but I couldn't care less. I just want to be alone.

My dad and mom have also been up my ass and lecturing me about not caring enough for Thalia. To be honest, I am just trying to forget about her.

She is probably on some island, enjoying being alone. She left because she was scared.

But there is no way in hell I am going to admit to Ace about Thalia and my activities before she left. If I did that then he would punch me until I'm black and blue.

I let out a groan before getting up from my bed and walking towards my shower. I turn the water on and change the temperature to make it cold.

I like taking cold showers in the morning because it wakes me up and it also relieves me sometimes when I need it.

Once I am done with my shower, I put a towel around my waist and walk towards my closet to find clothes to change into. Since I have a meeting with Ace and my parents, I have to dress a certain way which is kind of annoying.

Every time I have a meeting with them, they always tell me to dress formally which I don't understand. Every time I go to the meeting, Thalia never dresses formally. She always gets away with it but that's probably because her dad's in charge.

I change into a suit and tie before spraying cologne and leaving my room. Once I get outside, I pick my black Porsche 911 to drive to the De Luca estate. The car roars to life when I start the engine and then I pull out of my driveway and leave.

While driving, I listen to music while also thinking about what the hell this meeting could be for.

Did they find Thalia? Is it about the Russians?

So many fucking questions.

My mind has been kind of blank for the past few days. I have just been trying to distract myself so that I can stop thinking about Thalia. I don't want to think about her.

She hurt me when she decided to leave me instead of facing me. She is scared and for what?

Why would she be scared to face me? She never has been scared before so why now?

I swear that's all I have been thinking about. That's why I think she didn't get kidnapped by the Russians because Thalia knows how to take care of herself. She also would do something like run away from her problems and since I have known her, she has always been the one to do that.

It's just how Thalia rolls.

I get to the De Luca estate and park my car in the front after going through security. I get out of my car and walk inside the house and go to where Ace's office is.

I don't bother knocking because honestly, I don't give a fuck right now. I just want to go back home and be alone. I don't have time to find a girl who doesn't care about me.

"I remember telling you to knock, Alexander," Ace states.

He is sitting at his desk while looking down at his papers.

No one else is in his office, it's just him.

"I don't have time to wait around for you, Ace. What do you need?" I ask as I sit down in the chair in front of his desk.

"I know what happened. I found Thalia," Ace claims, making me raise my eyebrows.

"Well, where is she then?"

"Still in Russia. More specifically in the Ivanov estate." Ace looks up at me from his papers. "So now I am trying to figure out what the fuck happened and what you guys did wrong."

"What makes you think we did something wrong?" I ask in a bored tone.

He can't seriously be blaming me, can he?

"Alexander, you went with Thalia to Moscow. You were both supposed to come back together but I only see one of you in front of me. What happened while you two were in Russia, Alexander?

Why did Thalia leave without you?" Ace asks while placing his arms on his desk.

"I don't know. How about you ask her when you see her?" I say in a sarcastic tone.

"I would love to, but she isn't here, Alexander. Why did she leave?"

I roll my eyes. "I wish I knew the answer." Ace then lets out an annoyed sigh and rubs his forehead. "How do you know where she is?"

"I have a mole in their estate, and he heard Vladimir's men talking about how they have Thalia."

I clench my fist imagining everything that they could be doing to her.

She shouldn't have fucking left without me.

This is her fault. She did this to herself.

"What did Aria say?"

"I haven't told her yet. You are the first to know. I wanted to get a backstory from you but obviously, that won't happen," Ace says frustratedly.

"Look, I didn't do shit so stop blaming me and thinking that I did."

Ace then stands up from his chair and he looks down at me. "I would be very careful with how you act around me right now Alexander," Ace threatens. "You are going to help me find Thalia," Ace states coldly.

I chuckle. "The fuck I will."

Thalia hurt me. I am not going to help find her. It is her fault that she fucking left without me. She will deal with the consequences.

Ace furrows his eyebrows at me. "What did you just say? Did you say no to me?"

I stand up from my chair and lean closer to Ace. "I said the fuck I will. I am not helping you," I deadpan.

Suddenly I feel a punch to my face. I hold onto my jaw that is hurting and I look at Ace and see him glaring at me.

"You will help me, Alexander. I don't care about your little feud, but my daughter is gone. She isn't at home where she belongs so you will help me get her back if it's the last thing I do."

I chuckle again.

Shit, I might be a fucking lunatic for arguing with Ace De Luca out of all people, but I can't think straight right now.

"No."

I feel another punch to the face and before I can stop myself, I throw a punch to Ace's face making him hold his jaw.

Ace composes himself and then walks around the table to pin me down on the floor. "You are fucking crazy!" Ace yells and he punches me in the face again.

I throw a punch to Ace's face and another to his neck to get him off of me, but he doesn't.

The fuck?

Isn't a punch to the throat supposed to throw someone off or something?

"I didn't do shit. You shouldn't have assumed."

"Agree to help me, Alexander," Ace demands while sending another punch to my face, making my lip bleed.

I punch Ace in the face catching him off guard, so I throw him off of me and stand up. "Fuck you! I'm not helping!" I yell while Ace stands up and wipes the blood from his nose. "It's her fault she left, and I am not going to be there to pick up her mess. You are her dad so you can do that shit. I'm going home and if you call me again about her then I am not answering," I say, before walking away from Ace.

He lets me walk past him out the door. Once I get to my car, I ignore the throbbing pain in my head and just start driving.

Twenty Four

It's been almost a week and I still haven't eaten. My stomach hurts so much from how empty it feels.

I feel drained and weak. I feel like I want to faint, but I can't because if I do then who knows what the hell Vladimir can do to me or his men.

I don't want to take that risk so that's why I am still awake, trying so hard not to slip into unconsciousness.

I wonder what my family is thinking.

I wonder if they know where I am and if they are trying to save me.

I can't help but think about Alexander. I am also starting to feel bad for leaving and now I know I made a mistake by doing that. I should have just stayed until he woke up but instead, I acted like a scared bitch and left.

I hear talking from outside the hallway. The talking becomes more and more vivid. The door of my room opens but I don't bother looking up.

I hear a bag drop so I look across from me and see there is a plastic bag with food inside.

"Boss wants you to eat," I look up and see one of the guards. "Are you going to eat it or not?" he asks rudely.

"I would love to, but my hands are chained to the wall," I say in a raspy voice. It feels like a thousand tiny needles are stabbing my throat. The man walks forward, and he unchains one of my hands making it drop to the floor. I wince while stretching my hand. Fuck those chains were tight. I reach to grab the bag and as I get the food out the man still doesn't leave making me look up at him. "You need something?"

"Boss wants me to watch you eat to make sure you don't try anything."

I haven't seen Vladimir since our last encounter.

I honestly think he is scared of the little threat I gave him. It would make sense because he is a scared bitch.

Kind of like me.

But you see, I run away from problems that I don't want to face and that I am scared to face. But Vladimir is scared because of a small threat I made. Me, a little girl who is just the Italian Mafia princess.

I laugh at the thought before reaching inside the bag and getting out a bag of chips.

At least they are feeding me good food. So, I definitely can't complain.

As I am eating I feel the man's eyes on me making me a little uncomfortable. "Instead of having your eyes dead set on me can you maybe just look somewhere else?" I raise my eyebrow.

"Not what the boss told me to do," the man says, shrugging his shoulders.

"What's your name?" I ask while eating.

"Rowan," he states coldly as he watches me eat.

I look back up at him and take some time to admire his features.

He has dark brown hair that looks soft and makes me want to pull at the roots. His eyes are brown with some blue mixed in.

I admire his body and notice the strong tanned biceps underneath the black shirt he is wearing.

He screams familiar.

"Last name?" I ask.

"Valentino," he states in an Italian accent.

That's it.

Thank god, I am going to get out of here.

"Nice to meet you, Rowan," I smile. "What do you go by here?"

"Nicolas. But just letting you know that they are coming to get you."

"Oh, joy," I mutter. "What have I missed since I was gone?"

"Well, your father and Alexander had a fight but other than that they were just trying to find you."

I widen my eyes at Alexander's actions. "Why did they fight?"

"Alexander didn't want to help you," Rowan states calmly.

I roll my eyes. "He's a jackass. Didn't expect anything less."

Although I did feel a pang to my heart. I was hoping Alexander would be here to come in and save me but I guess not. "When did you arrive?"

"A few days ago. Your father assigned me to watch over you and make sure that nothing too bad happens," Rowan states.

"Well, I appreciate it."

"They are coming though. I have a feeling Alexander will as well."

"He is an ass. I don't think he is coming," I chuckle.

I say that, yet my mind can't help but repeat in my head over and over that Alexander didn't want to help me.

Rowan stands up. "You never know. That boy is in love with you, but he might not know it."

I narrow my eyes at Rowan. "I don't think so."

Rowan comes forward and chains my hand to the wall once I am finished eating. "We will see." He picks up the trash that is on the floor and looks back at me before leaving. "Try not to argue. Just stay quiet and make sure to keep your mouth shut. It will help if you don't get another cut on your lip."

I smile at Rowan. "I'll try."

Rowan leaves and now I am left alone in the dark again.

Thank fucking god they are coming. It shouldn't be long now.

Right?

Twenty Five

It's been probably about a week since the fight with Ace happened. He has called me countless times and so has Aria and my parents. I haven't answered any of them though.

I have just been alone in my house, avoiding everyone. I just don't feel like talking to anyone.

But today I have to go to the De Luca estate because I have to babysit Killian.

He is almost fucking sixteen years old and he doesn't know how to take care of himself?

Ace sent one of his men to my house so that they could tell me. They said that Killian was apparently grounded, and they don't want him sneaking out or anything so now I'm stuck babysitting that fucker.

I pull into the De Luca residence and park my car in the front. I am just getting Killian and then we are leaving 'cause I'm not staying here.

I walk inside the house and close the door behind me. I hear a phone going off in the kitchen, so I walk towards there and see Killian who is resting his head on the counter as he sits in one of the stool chairs in front of the island.

His phone is ringing but he makes no move to pick it up.

I walk towards him and bring his head up, holding his hair.

He looks like a fucking mess.

I let go of his hair making his head fall back on the counter.

"Ow, you jackass!" Killian whines and then brings his head up to look at me. "That fucking hurt."

"What the fuck is wrong with you?" I ask harshly.

"Isn't it obvious?" Killian raises his eyebrow and looks at me. "I'm hungover," Killian sneers.

I shake my head lightly and walk to the fridge. I open the door and grab two water bottles. I hand one to Killian and he takes a sip out of it.

"What did you do last night?" I ask before leaning against the kitchen counter across from Killian.

"Went to this party with my friends. I was still grounded for sneaking out on your guy's birthday."

"Who grounded you? Aria or Ace?"

"My dad. He saw me sneaking back inside my room when he was crossing the hall," Killian says while rubbing his head. "Fuck, I shouldn't have drank that much whisky."

God, Killian looks like a fucking mess.

I have never seen him so, what's the word?

Fucked up?

"You good?" I ask while raising my eyebrow at him.

Killian looks up at me and then smiles. "Better than ever," he says in a sarcastic tone at the same time I hear the doorbell ring.

"You expecting anyone?"

"Nope."

"Get your shit ready. We're going to my house," I say before walking out of the kitchen and down the hall to the front door.

I open the door and see Cameron.

What the fuck is Cameron doing here? Didn't Thalia end things with this fucker.

God, I want to punch his face so bad.

"Hey, Alexander, right?" Cameron asks and I lean against the door frame and raise my eyebrows at him.

"What do you want?"

"Is Thalia home?"

I clench my fist and jaw and trail my eyes down his body.

God, he still dresses like a fucking teenager.

Pathetic.

He looks way too fucking safe.

Why would Thalia go for a guy like him?

"Why?"

"I need to talk to her. She hasn't been answering any of my calls."

"So, you come to her house like a fucking stalker?" I ask bluntly.

I see Cameron clench his fist and he lets out an annoyed sigh.

Oh yea, pretty boy, punch me in the face.

See what happens.

"Look, I just need to talk to her."

"She doesn't want to talk to you," I deadpan.

Cameron furrows his eyebrows and then glares at me.

"Look, I have no clue what you are to her but you sure as hell aren't her boyfriend or dad or brother. So, whatever you say doesn't mean shit to me. Move out of the way and let me talk to her," Cameron takes a step closer to me, but I just stare at him trying not to laugh.

"One of those statements is wrong but it doesn't matter," I say quickly. "But she doesn't want to see you anymore. She doesn't like you. All you were to Thalia was a fuck, nothing more. Go find some other bitch to put your dick in 'cause Thalia doesn't want yours."

"The fuck you mean. You don't know shit!" he yells and I roll my eyes before leaning off the door and towering over him.

"I am not going to repeat myself," I state while glaring at him. "Either you leave willingly or I will make you and trust me you don't want to piss me off right now." I close the door in his face and rub my forehead.

Cameron.

Out of all people.

I remember Cameron. He is a cliché golden boy from high school.

Never thought Thalia would go for a guy like that. He is just so, what's the word?

Weak.

And he put his dick in her like what the hell?

What was she thinking?

Is she that stupid?

I walk back inside the kitchen and see Killian still sitting there.

"Why don't you like him?" Killian asks.

"'Cause he isn't like us. He is weak. I don't know why your sister ever went out with him."

"Maybe because she wanted someone else, but she couldn't have him," Killian chuckles. "Fucking cliché."

I furrow my eyebrows at him. "The fuck you mean? Who?"

Killian lifts his head to look at me. "Ask Jane. Maybe she will tell you." Killian stands from the island. "How long am I staying at yours?"

"Just today. But I need to text your dad to make sure."

No way in fucking hell is she going to be having anyone.

Only me.

"I thought you weren't talking to my dad?"

"Well, now I am. I need to find your sister," I say and get my phone out of my pocket. "Get your shit. Hurry up because I don't have the time or patience to be waiting for you."

Twenty Six

Rowan has been coming into my room every other day to feed me and make sure I am still breathing.

I have gotten a little of my strength back, but I still feel weaker than normal. My arms fucking hurt like a bitch too since they are still chained to the wall, and I haven't had a decent night's rest in such a long time.

I have been rotting in this damn room for almost two weeks.

Fuck I can't wait to go home and go to sleep. I have been daydreaming about my bed and what it feels like.

I have also been doing a lot of thinking about a lot of things which is kind of scary. I have been thinking about Alexander, my parents, the marriage, the whole mafia, and then what Vladimir's plan could be.

Speaking of him, I still haven't talked to him or seen him. The last time I saw him was when I first came here and when I threatened him.

I think I definitely scared him with my threat because-

"How is my little princess doing?"

My thinking gets cut off when I hear his voice. I look up and see Vladimir.

When the fuck did he get here?

I roll my eyes and look back down at the floor. "What can I do for you, Vladimir?"

"You know things are starting to come into motion."

"With what?" I narrow my eyes at him.

"My plan. My plan for your family's fall. Where your entire world crumbles in the palm of my hand."

"Sure," I chuckle.

One way I have been entertaining myself is fucking around with the guards outside my room. They are told not to touch me no matter how much I fuck with them or bug them. But now that Vladimir is here, I can threaten him again.

Vladimir walks closer to me and then kneels, so his face is right in front of mine. "You have such a big mouth. I wonder how your lover Alexander takes care of that or your father."

"And I bet you have a small dick just like every other douche bag on this planet." I then feel Vladimir grab my hair and pull me so close that I can feel his breath hit my face. "Get the fuck out of my face, do you have a decent toothpaste or something?" I groan as he holds onto my hair tighter.

I then feel a hand slap my face harshly. "What the fuck is wrong with you?"

I chuckle. "A lot of things." I look at Vladimir and see him glaring at me. "Let me go," I demand.

Vladimir gets closer to my face, and I can feel his lips touch mine making me back up a little and almost gag from him being this close to me.

"Before I kill you, I am going to for sure teach you how to show some fucking respect," he sneers and he is about to say something else but then we hear noises from outside the door making Vladimir look the other way. "What the fuck?"

I headbutt him and then kick him in the dick making him groan and let go of my hair.

I feel myself smile a little bit. "You're fucked now," I state as he keeps holding his balls.

The door of the room opens, and I see a man walk inside the room. "Thank fucking god," the man says. He sounds so familiar and calming. His voice makes me feel safe. The man kicks Vladimir in the face and then takes out what looks like a knife and then stabs him in the chest dragging the knife downwards making blood come out of his body. The man stands up and he walks closer to me, and I realize that it's Alexander. God, I have never been so happy to see him in my life. Alexander kneels in front of me, and he takes my face in his hands. "God, we need to get you out of here," he says while trailing his eyes all over my face.

Do I smell bad?

I really hope I don't because if I do then that would be so embarrassing and gross.

"No shit, Sherlock," I say sarcastically, and Alexander rolls his eyes then unlocks the chains around my hands, making them fall to the floor.

Alexander picks me up by my legs and stands up making him hold me bridal style.

"Don't worry everything is going to be alright now," Alexander whispers and he carries me out of the room.

His voice makes my heart feel like it is about to explode and in a good way this time.

"You don't have to hold me," I say and rest my head on his shoulder.

"I want to."

"Is Vladimir dead?" I ask softly.

"Yea, I carved my initials in his chest. Now quiet, we need to find a way out of here."

Alexander makes a lot of twists and turns as I just stare around him. I see a lot of cages and dead bodies on the floor. It looks like I was being held in a basement. There are metal cages and stone walls everywhere.

As Alexander walks through the house, I feel his breathing pick up. His body is warm while holding mine and I finally feel the sense of being safe and having no worries.

"I think I saw someone over here!" I hear someone yell.

Alexander makes a move to hide behind a wall and he looks back and forth between the two hallways.

Alexander then looks down at me. "Can you walk or stand?" I nod my head. "Okay, wait right here I need to go and kill the rest of the people in the house," he says before walking away, not letting me say anything.

I peek around the corner and see Alexander stab a couple of guys in the head and chest before pulling out his gun and shooting them.

I see a guy creep towards him, but Alexander is busy cutting out a guy's throat.

God, he never likes to do simple deaths like just cutting their neck, making them drop dead or stabbing them where it will just be quick and easy. He has to make it all extra and shit.

I get out of my hiding spot and trip the guy who is trying to kill Alexander. He falls to the ground, and I stomp on his face, making him wince. Alexander turns around and he kneels to look at the guy I stomped on. Alexander takes his gun and shoots the guy in the face.

He turns to glare at me. "What's that look for? I saved your life," I exclaim.

Alexander walks closer to me and picks me up by my legs. "I told you to wait," Alexander then carries me over his shoulder.

I punch his back and try to get him to drop me. "You dick! I can walk!"

"We'll have to change that soon, angel," he says before he walks outside.

Twenty Seven

I hear footsteps outside the door walking closer and closer. I also hear people talking in hushed whispers.

I open my eyes and look around the room I am in. I am laying on a bed with white covers. I open the window blinds next to me and I see the beautiful blue sky and white fluffy clouds.

The door of the room I am in opens and I turn my head and see Alexander walking in. He is wearing a white dress shirt that has some buttons undone and blood on the front of the shirt.

"Sorry if I woke you," Alexander says as he walks fully inside the room and closes the door behind him.

"It's fine," I turn my body around so that I can face him. "What time is it?"

Alexander sat on the end of the bed next to my legs. "3:00 am."

"What happened?"

Last thing I remember is Alexander bringing me to the car and then me falling asleep.

"They're dead."

"All of them?" I furrow my eyebrows.

"For now. You dad still needs to do some other things to make sure they are all for sure dead."

"How?"

"Your dad had a mole inside the Ivanov estate, and he figured out where you were. He sent Rowan to watch over you until he figured out a good plan."

"And what was that?"

Alexander chuckles lightly. "He did want to blow up the estate as he did twenty years ago but you were inside the estate, and he couldn't really do that or else you would be dead. So, he sent me to come and get you and some other men to kill off anyone who was in the estate and after we got out he blew up the estate. He is still trying to find out if there are more family members or anyone who is associated with their mafia."

"Where are my mom and dad?"

"They're in the room next to us."

I let out a sigh of relief that they are okay and alive. I don't know why, but I was so scared, thinking about whether or not I would get out of there or not. I had been there for two weeks and I was starting to doubt some things but I knew that my mom and dad would come and get me.

But I do wish I could have made my threat to Vladimir true.

I look up at Alexander and I see him staring straight at me. I feel nervous under his stare and just around him in general.

I also feel anxious and scared because of what happened between us.

I mean it was just sex though.

Right?

"Thank you," I say softly.

Alexander sigh and his hand comes to rest on my cheek. "You fucking scared me, Thalia," he says while looking down at me with a soft and adoring look. "I don't know what I would have done if I found out you were dead."

"I thought you didn't care. Rowan said-"

"I was pissed off you left," Alexander says, cutting me off. "I didn't want to face the fact that you leaving me that morning hurt when it did."

"You are the type who does these kinds of things so I thought if I left then things would have been easier."

Alexander furrows his eyebrows at me. "You really think that Thalia?"

"It's what you're known for."

Right when I said it, I immediately regretted saying it.

Alexander takes his hand off my cheek, and all the warmth that I felt in my body leaves, and I'm left with the cold, lonely feeling.

"Thanks for that," Alexander stands up and I grab his hand.

"I didn't mean it like that."

"Yeah, but you said it."

Alexander lets go of my hand and walks out of the room, leaving me alone.

Twenty Eight

It's been a week since we got back from Moscow.

I have been on bed rest because my mom and dad think that I should rest. My mom also had the cook make me a shit ton of food because she said I look way too skinny and that I should get food in my system.

It feels good to sleep in my bed again. I have gotten pretty decent sleep for most of the day.

Jane was also here when my dad, mom, and I arrived home. She was happy to see me. She has been coming over for the past few days to check up on me.

Believe it or not, Killian was also happy and relieved to see me in one piece. But when I saw him, he looked so different.

He looked kind of fucked up and not in a good way. I tried to talk to him to see if he was okay, but he just replied with a sarcastic comment. But I am going to talk to him about it because he just looks so hurt and broken. I don't know what it could be about because Killian and I barely talk to each other.

But for the past week, I just have been on bed rest and being a lazy ass. I miss going to the gym though, so I decide to go use the gym in the house today.

I quickly change into a pair of leggings and then a long sleeve cropped top. I put on a pair of black converse. I tie my hair up in a ponytail and leave my room to walk towards the gym.

I probably shouldn't be working out, but I need my strength.

As I walk towards the gym, I hear sounds coming from where the gym is located. I turn the corner and see a lot of men inside the gym taking apart the walls and punching bags. They look like they are construction workers.

"Um, what's going on?"

"Ms. De Luca," one of them says before taking off his hat. He walks towards me. "Your father requested that we move the gym to the other side of the yard because of the redesign."

I furrow my eyebrows. "Do you know where he is?"

"I believe he is still in his office."

"Thank you," I smile at him before walking back inside the house, towards my father's office.

I open the door and see my dad talking to someone. He diverts his eyes away from the guy and then back at me. The guy looks kind of familiar but I wouldn't know because his back is facing me.

He looks back at the guy. "That's all for now. Thank you again, Rowan. You did a good job," my dad says.

"Of course, sir," Rowan says and then turns around. "Thalia," Rowan nods. "I'm glad to see that you're healthy."

I smile. "Thank you. I'm glad to see you are getting recognition."

Rowan smirks before saying goodbye and leaving out the door.

I smile and watch him walk out of the door.

"How are you feeling *la mia principessa*?"

I look at my dad and walk to sit in the chair in front of his desk. "Better. I was just going to go workout but the workers outside said you are moving the gym."

"Yea, I just want to get started on the redesign. It will give us more space in the gym since I want to put in the boxing ring there."

After a few days of resting my dad came inside my room to talk about how stupid I was when I left without Alexander. He told me not to do something like that again.

"Oh."

"Why? Were you going to go work out or something?"

"Yeah, I wanted to get back in the gym and start working out and training again."

"The gym won't be done till the end of the week. You can go use Alexander's gym. I know his gym is big enough for the both of you."

The problem with that is Alexander and I haven't talked since the day we left Moscow. He hasn't come to the house, and I haven't made any move to talk to him.

We still have yet to talk about the wedding but I'm hoping that if I don't bring it up then we hopefully won't move forward with it.

"Alexander's gym?" I repeat and raise my eyebrows.

My dad looks up at me. "What's the issue?"

"It's Alexander," I deadpan.

"And?" My dad stares at me and raises his eyebrow. "I still don't see the issue, Thalia."

I let out an annoyed sigh. "I just don't want to see him."

My dad rolls his eyes. "This little feud between you two has to stop. Go."

"Dad-"

"I said go, Thalia, before I drag you there myself," my dad cuts me off and looks back down at his papers on his desk.

I refrain from arguing and I get out of my chair and walk out of his office.

I really really don't want to go but I also really need to go to the gym.

Damn it.

I walk out of the front door and go to where my car is parked. Once I get inside the car I drive out of the estate and down the street.

I really don't feel like facing him or just being near him.

Call me a wimp, but Alexander is the one person I am scared of. Something about him just makes me weak, mentally and physically. And now that we have had sex it's even scarier and it makes me feel even more vulnerable to him.

The drive to Alexander's house isn't long. His security lets me in, and I park next to one of his many sports cars.

I will never understand why he is so obsessed with cars, he has over twenty different cars while I only have two. One of the cars, which is a white Ferrari, is a gift my mom and dad gave me for my birthday. My other car is the one I bought myself, it's a black Porsche 911 which is my favorite car.

I walk to his front door and open it. I walk inside and smell bacon and eggs.

Damn.

I also hear music playing from the kitchen, so I walk towards the kitchen and when I do I see Alexander wearing just black boxer briefs while cooking eggs and bacon in separate pans.

He wasn't dancing or singing, just mumbling the words while focusing on the food.

I try my best not to stare at his body.

I walk more inside the kitchen. "I thought you were more of a pancake guy?"

Alexander looks at me and I see something flash in his eyes before it disappears.

He looks back at his food. "What are you doing here?"

"I am here to use your gym 'cause ours is under construction I guess." I walk to the fridge and open it.

"Oh, joy," he mutters.

Alexander turns off the stove and then puts his food on the plate next to him.

I grab a water bottle and then close the fridge. I turn around and see Alexander standing right in front of me.

I take a sip of water before twisting the cap on. "Yea?"

"What are you doing here Thalia?" Alexander whispers and then leans his face closer to mine.

"Going to work out, Alexander."

Alexander then smirks at me and trails his eyes down my body.

I felt like my body was on fucking fire.

"We can do that and so much more, Thalia."

He leans closer to me and I back away from him. "We aren't doing this again, Alexander," I claim.

Alexander leans closer to my face. "Tell me to stop then."

Alexander comes closer and closer, and I still don't make any move to stop him or move away.

But finally, I feel his lips capture mine.

Twenty Nine

I DON'T MOVE ONCE HIS LIPS ARE ON MINE.

I feel Alexander's hands slide onto my waist and he pulls me closer to him. My lips start to move against his and I trail my hands to his biceps.

Alexander tries to slide his tongue in but I don't let him. He bites my lips making me moan and my mouth opens a little bit. He slides his tongue in and fights for dominance.

I feel his hands slide down to my hips and then I remember what the hell I am doing.

I remove my lips from his. "No, we can't," I say while trying to fix my breathing.

Alexander leans his forehead on mine. "Tell me why? What's wrong with us doing this?"

"So many things. Like one, Cameron."

"Took care of him, angel."

I furrow my eyebrows at him. "What do you mean? You didn't kill him, did you?"

"No, but he doesn't like you anymore," Alexander shrugs. He leans closer to me. "You can't keep lying to yourself saying that you don't want this." Alexander presses his hips into mine and sure enough I can feel his bulge.

I remember he is wearing briefs so I can feel everything.

It's not that I don't, it's just that I am scared. I have seen what love is like and I don't want to go through that.

But when I look at my mom and dad, I believe that love or relationships are real. But relationships, in general, are scary and I don't want to get my heart broken.

If I do this with Alexander, he will just break my heart.

I narrow my eyes at Alexander. "I hate you. That is the only thing I am thinking."

Alexander then smiles.

He fucking smiles.

"Angry sex is the best kind of sex," Alexander says before placing his lips on mine again and picking me up by my legs.

I don't make any movements to pull away from him.

Alexander rubs my thighs as he walks through the house, and I trail my kisses down his neck.

He opens the door and walks towards his bed before placing me down. His lips are back on mine, and I reach to grab his face to pull him closer to me if that's even possible. His hands are rubbing the sides of my body.

I just can't get enough of this feeling.

"Xander," I whisper.

I feel Alexander's bulge against me, and he starts to kiss down my neck. "I need you so bad," he whispers against my skin.

I squeeze my thighs together, the uncomfortable feeling I am getting in between my thighs makes me want to pull down his briefs and pull his hips into mine. "Please," I beg without knowing what the fuck I am begging for.

Alexander lifts his head and makes a move to take off my clothes. I am now bare naked in front of him, and his eyes trail all the way down my body. "Fucking beautiful." Alexander leans down and I feel his lips touch my breast making me close my eyes.

Alexander licks and sucks my breasts, pulling at the piercing while groping the other before flipping us over making me sit on his lap.

I moan as I rub myself against him, closing my eyes pretending he is inside me.

God, I want him.

Alexander kisses me as he takes off his boxer briefs. Once I feel his hot flesh against mine, I moan and shut my eyes tightly.

I feel him slip in before slipping back out. "Baby," I whimper and hold on to him.

He removes his lips from mine and puts them on my breast. "God, you're so beautiful, angel." His tongue starts playing with my metal piercing and I shiver. "Put it in," he huskily demands, grabbing my ass. I look down and grab his cock, pumping him a few times before sliding it in between my legs. "Holy shit," his eyes roll back.

I whimper as I inch further down his cock. Alexander throws his head back once I am filled with him.

God, this sight of him beneath me just makes me let go already.

I grip onto his muscular shoulders and lift myself off of him and then sink back down. Feeling Alexander deep inside, my stomach churns and twists. I begin to bounce up and down on his cock, fucking the both of us into oblivion.

Alexander groans as his hands make their way to my thighs helping me move.

I start to feel pleasure burning in my body, moving me closer and closer to my climax. "Feels so good," I whisper.

Then he clamps his hands down on my hips, stopping me from moving anymore.

I try to move off of him, but he stops me and holds me down. "Ah ah," he tsked at me when I tried to move. "Stay down."

"Xand-"

"Stay down, angel," he says in a voice that screams dominance, reminding me who is in charge. Asshole. "Take it all."

I whimper as I feel him inside my stomach, and I try to move again while still whimpering trying to get off.

Alexander makes eye contact with me, and his own hips thrust upward, hitting my g-spot. I let out a loud moan while he fucks me to the point where my toes start to curl. I try to move off of him, from how overwhelming this all is, but he keeps his arms tightly wrapped around me.

He then flips us around so that I am on my back, and he is on top of me.

"I'm close." I reach down and start to rub my clit.

Alexander bits his lip while watching me and pounding inside of me. My legs start to shake as I yell his name.

"That's right angel, scream my name."

I make a move to grab the pillow behind me but instead, Alexander takes both of my hands and pins them above my head.

Alexander leans down and sucks on different spots on my neck as I wrap my legs around his waist.

"Xander!" I blurt as he hits a new angle and makes me feel all of the pleasure rush through my body.

Alexander lets go of my arms and I can't help but hold onto him. I claw his back and yell his name repeatedly. Alexander doesn't stop, he continues pounding into me relentlessly. But when he finally does climax with me, he shuts his eyes and lets out a moan as he comes.

Thirty

The first thing I see when I open my eyes is the sunlight shining through the window that is open across from the bed.

I squint my eyes and look around the room. I realize I am in Alexander's room and all the memories of yesterday come back. We legit spent most of yesterday afternoon and night fucking each other into oblivion.

God, stupid stupid stupid.

How many more times until I understand?

The first time should have been enough.

But it's like something draws me closer to him and I want him to make me feel good and in a way only he makes me feel.

He makes me feel like my stomach always has butterflies and then when he touches me I feel like my whole body is on fire.

I sit up in his bed and look around the room. I don't see him anywhere, instead I smell bacon and eggs.

I get up from his bed and look for my clothes that are folded on the chair by his window. While changing, the spot between my legs starts to ache, a whole fucking lot.

Damnit.

Once I change into my leggings and shirt I walk out of his room after opening a window because it was kind of starting to smell like sweat and sex.

When I eventually walk inside the kitchen I see Alexander cooking food in the pan with only a pair of briefs on.

I'm getting deja vu from yesterday.

"Hello," I state and walk to the stools he has in front of his island.

Alexander turns to look at me and then goes back to cooking. "Morning."

I look at Alexander while he cooks. I also see how his back tenses up and I study his tattoos on his back.

I remember Alexander telling me that he wants to get his whole upper body tatted. I thought he was crazy because it looks like it hurts but that was when we were teenagers, now I don't really feel pain when getting a tattoo.

I don't know what Alexander is going to do with the rest of the space on his body, 'cause that's a lot of space and he only has a few tattoos.

"Done staring?"

I ignore his comment and try not to feel embarrassed. "When are you getting more tattoos?"

Alexander grabs a plate filled with eggs and another plate filled with bacon. "Want some?

"Sure," I shrug and he hands me the plate and then sits down next to me.

I serve myself some eggs and bacon and so does he.

"I am getting more soon. I would get multiple tattoos at once but I want to make sure I like how the placement looks."

"What are you thinking about getting next?"

Alexander chuckles. "You'll see. You have to wait like everyone else."

I roll my eyes and focus on eating what's on my plate.

I know for a fact that we might have to talk about the elephant in the room. Being this close to him, feeling his body heat radiate onto mine makes me feel crazy.

Alexander gets up from his chair once he is done eating and he takes our plates to the sink.

"So, I think we should talk," I state while Alexander does the dishes.

"About?" Alexander asks without looking at me.

"Yesterday," I say. "I'm not the type of person to fuck around, Alexander and whatever this is, it needs to stop."

Alexander then turns around and furrows his eyebrows. "Why does it need to stop?"

"Because I am not the type to just kiss people and then have one-night stands."

"Thalia, you know that is not what we are."

Then what the fuck are we?

I don't want to be fuck buddies.

"We aren't anything. I hate you and you hate me, remember?" I state.

Alexander rolls his eyes. "You are so fucking stupid," he

mutters.

I narrow my eyes at Alexander and stand up from the stool I am sitting on. "What did you just say?"

Alexander looks directly at me. "I said you're fucking stupid. You are stupid, scared, weak, and a fucking pussy. You won't ever be the leader that your father is. You're going to make the entire mafia fall," he spits.

I feel my body burn with something.

What the fuck is it?

Hate?

Hurt?

I take a step towards Alexander and then slap him across the face. "You don't know shit," I say while trying not to let a tear fall. "You're such an asshole. You're mad because I don't want to have sex with you. Do you know the kind of people who act like that? Children. Children throw a tantrum and whine when they don't get something they want. You, Xander, are a fucking child," I state before walking out of his kitchen and towards the front door.

I wipe a tear that falls as I walk to my car. Once I get inside, I start the car and drive onto the street, away from Alexander.

This is what I was afraid of.

I liked the way Alexander made me feel and because of that, he hurt me. Alexander just wants someone to fuck. He doesn't like me. He doesn't do feelings and shit.

Why would he?

I don't like him. I like the way he makes me feel. Two different things.

I hate him.

Just like he hates me.

Thirty One

This is probably a stupid idea but when have I ever been the type to not have stupid ideas?

Currently I am walking into a mansion full of people that are drinking, smoking, doing drugs, and probably playing games that will end up making you question what kind of person you are in the morning.

I'm also walking inside the house with Rowan, out of all people.

As Rowan and I walk inside the house, multiple pairs of eyes look our way. Who wouldn't?

Rowan is tall, strong, and looks like sex on legs while I'm an attractive girl with a black lacy dress on that probably shows everyone how my ass looks.

"So, this is what you do when you're not getting kidnapped by Russians?" Rowan whispers in my ear as he grabs my hand and walks us towards the kitchen where the drinks are all laid out.

"That's right. Partying until I feel like throwing up in the morning."

"Why'd you decide to bring me?" Rowan asks as he walks inside the kitchen.

He leans on the counter while I pour a drink.

"Because you interest me."

"How so?"

I look at Rowan and admire him for a few seconds. His arms are crossed over his chest, and he has a serious look on his face. He almost looks emotionless as he stares at me.

Like a corpse that feels nothing.

I bet if the most gorgeous girl, or even me, walked up to him and started flirting with him, he probably wouldn't feel a thing.

I feel like it would take a lot for Rowan to crack or at least show some sort of emotion.

"Because you're very stoic. You don't really show any emotion. Anger, sadness, annoyance, anxiety, anticipation, or even interest. Especially when I'm standing next to you."

"There is nothing in the world that has captured my attention yet, Thalia. You're a beautiful girl but not for me."

"Interesting," I smile and nod my head at him before taking a sip of my drink.

I offer Rowan a drink, but he shakes his head and says he's good.

While talking to Rowan a little more, my eyes catch a familiar form walking through the house.

Alexander is wearing a white t-shirt with black trousers and that gold chain with a cross around his neck, like the fucking stud he is.

I haven't spoken to him since the day in his house which was almost a week ago.

The past week I have been distracting myself with wedding preparations, trying not to think about Alexander Russo and how I feel with him.

Ever since I left his house, my body has been feeling needy and desperate for something. I hate the way it's making me feel and I hate that Alexander is the only one who can take that feeling away and replace it with something better.

I was hoping Rowan would help me out tonight, but I don't see that happening anymore.

I don't think Rowan would even kiss me if I begged him on my knees for it. He seems like the type to only fuck when he is with girls. No kissing or intimate touches.

I bet he fucks good though.

"What's up with you and Russo?"

My eyes go back to Rowan and that feeling in my stomach washes away.

"What do you mean?" I raise my eyebrow at him.

"You and Alexander. Everyone sees it."

"Sees what?"

"How you two want each other."

I can't help but chuckle.

"We don't want each other."

Rowan nods his head lightly. "Come here."

I raise an eyebrow at Rowan. "Why?"

"Stop asking questions and come here," Rowan demands, in a rougher tone that made me feel butterflies in my stomach. I walk towards Rowan until I'm standing in front of him. "Close your eyes." I do as he says and close my eyes. I feel a light touch on my shoulder, making my skin break out in goosebumps. "Now imagine yourself bare on a bed with silk sheets. A specific bed with a specific someone above you, running their finger down your body." Rowan's finger travels down. Alexander flashes in my head when Rowan drags his finger over my stomach. "That spot between your legs is pulsing and you can't help but rub your thighs together as you imagine everything that he will do to you." Rowan's finger travels down my stomach until it grazes the spot between my legs. "What's his name, Thalia?" Rowan whispers in my ear.

My head leans back as I say, "Xander." My hips lean closer to Rowan's hand, but Rowan pushes me away from him softly, making me open my eyes. Rowan's eyebrow is lifted, and his head is tilted to the side. "You're a jerk."

"Just proving a point," Rowan shrugs his shoulders and his eyes travel to whatever is behind me. "And looks like your lover is on his way to claim what's his." Rowan leans off the wall and is about to walk past me, but his lips are next to my ear again. "I'll wait in the car. If you don't come out in an hour or so, then I'm leaving you here."

I watch Rowan pass everyone in the hallway and walk towards the front door. As he leaves, I feel a hand grab my wrist and pull me away from the kitchen. I look at who is pulling me, and I see Alexander.

"What the fuck is wrong with you? Let go," I demand but Alexander ignores me and pulls me through the crowd of people. I let Alexander pull me through the crowd until we end up in a dark bedroom. Alexander lets go of my hand and he walks around the room, pacing like a fucking maniac. "So, are you going to tell me why you decided to drag me inside of some bedroom?"

Alexander finally faces me, and I swear I feel like my heart flips as he looks at me like he wants to commit the biggest sin on me.

"You have a thing for pissing me off, don't you? Do you get off on it or something?" Alexander asks as he walks closer to me.

I shrug my shoulders. "Maybe a little."

"I can tell." Alexander's hand slides onto my waist. "What were you and that fucker Rowan talking about? He seemed really close to you."

"You always have to worry about what I do with other people don't you?" I raise my eyebrow at him, and Alexander just has the audacity to smirk. "Maybe we were talking about how annoying your face is sometimes."

"Thalia, if I'm so annoying when why are you dripping wet right now?"

I can't help but press my thighs together.

How would he know?

"Ew. No." I grimace, but then feel Alexander's hand slide up my thigh and I feel his hand cup me. He can definitely feel how wet I am through my underwear.

My eyes close and I can't help but let a small moan escape from my lips.

"Seem pretty fucking wet to me, angel," Alexander whispers in my ear. I don't say anything. Instead, I grind into his hand that isn't moving, just pressing against me. "Oh yea, little Thalia is wet for me."

"Xander-" I get cut off by Alexander pressing his lips against mine. One of his fingers moves my underwear to the side and he slips a finger inside me making my grip on him tighten. The kiss is filled with something desirable and desperate. I want to feel his skin on mine and then the heat of his body surrounding me. I want more of him. "I guess your face isn't that bad," I mutter before nipping his bottom lip.

Alexander smiles against the kiss. "You want to sit on it?"

I can't help but smile and kiss him with urgency.

"You're so bipolar sometimes. It pisses me off."

Alexander takes his hand out from under my dress and then he leans back so we aren't kissing anymore.

"And you make me fucking crazy, Thalia. You might pretend or try and hide it from yourself, but I know you, Thalia," Alexander says, as his breathing slows down. "I know what you want. You want someone to love you but also excite you in ways no one else ever can. You want someone to challenge you to make things more interesting. To keep you on your toes and get your heart beating so fucking fast you won't even know what to do. I know everything about you, Thalia."

And even though my heart feels like it's just going to rip my chest open and offer itself to Alexander, I still manage to pretend for another few seconds that Alexander Russo means nothing to me.

Thirty Two

I try calling Cameron for the fifth time today, but he doesn't answer.

I just want to know what the fuck Alexander said to him. I want to make sure that he is okay and that he doesn't think I'm a heartless bitch, but he isn't answering.

I mean maybe it's for the best, I do need to drop him, but I wanted to do it on my terms. I wanted to make sure that we would at least be friends or acquaintances because Cameron is a good person and I wish that we would remain friends.

I have a meeting with my parents soon. My dad said that he wants to talk to Alexander and me.

After Alexander exposed me, I left him alone in the room and went to Rowan who was still waiting for me in the car. He was smart enough to not question me or say anything. I can tell he wanted to ask but he didn't.

Alexander hasn't called me or texted me which is good because I need space to breathe and be away from him for a little while.

Obviously, that's not going to work because we have to have a meeting with one another today, probably to discuss the wedding.

I do want to talk to my father about my role as the future capo.

I don't want to sound spoiled or anything because I am grateful for everything I have but I have always wanted to do what my father does. He looks so powerful and content with what he is doing. I have also been in his office for some meetings, and I like how demanding my dad is. I want to do that. But obviously not in a mean way, in a badass bitch kind of way.

But Alexander thinks I would fail.

I still haven't forgotten what he said. It hurts when I think about it but it's better not to talk to Alexander about that or how he made me feel.

I am going to take over the mafia just like I have always wanted to.

I walk out of my room, and I look at Killian's room before passing it.

He just seems so different, and he looks sad. I have never seen my brother sad before. He has always been either douchey or energetic. He likes to mess around with people and tease them, but now he is just always in his room and has a bad attitude.

He has a sad look in his eyes. And for some reason I have a feeling things for him are about to get a whole lot harder.

I look at his door one more time before walking to my dad's office. I walk in and see my dad on the phone.

"Don't worry *amore* everything will be fine. I will make sure of it," my dad assured. I knock on the door and he looks up at me. "Thalia just got here for the meeting. I'll see you in a little bit. Drive safe alright?" my dad asks in a soft tone. "I love you."

My dad hangs up and puts his phone on the desk before looking at me.

"Was that mom?" I ask when I sit down on the chair in front of his desk.

"Yea. She went to the mall with Emma to buy something for Val and Mia."

I furrow my eyebrows. "Val and Mia are coming over?"

Val and Mia are my aunt and uncle, not by blood, but they are very close to my dad. Mia is a journalist in America and Val has been traveling all over the world, so I haven't really heard from him.

"Yes."

"Why?"

"I will tell you in a little but let's wait for Alexander."

Suspicious but okay.

Then I remember Killian.

"I think something is wrong with Killian," I claim. My dad looks up at me. "He hasn't been acting the same since I left. Did something happen?"

My dad takes his hands off the computer and turns to look at me. "I don't know. I tried talking to him, but he doesn't want to talk. I know something happened though."

"What do you think happened?"

My dad lets out a sigh. "No clue but you're right, he doesn't seem like himself."

"I can try talking to him," I offer.

My dad nods his head. "Make sure it's soon though because his birthday is coming up and I want him to be happy you know?" My dad and Killian don't have the best relationship. Killian always likes to challenge my dad and then argues with him about everything. I have a feeling that Killian and my dad are going to have a lot of issues when he gets older. I nod my head at the same time we hear a knock on the door. "Come in."

The door opens and I already know that it's Alexander who walks in. I don't make any moves to look at him, I just stare straight at my father.

"What do you need?" Alexander asks as he sits next to me in the chair.

My dad lets out a frustrated sigh and looks at the papers on his desk. "In a week, your wedding is going to happen."

"A week? I thought that was going to be farther out. Maybe summer?" I question.

"No. I want to get this done as fast as possible."

"Why? We already dealt with the Russians. Do we even need to have a wedding?"

"Yes. It would be better if we joined the mafias again. I don't like the threat that Russia made with our family and even though they are dealt with, that doesn't mean that other groups won't threaten us."

"I don't think it's necessary," Alexander argued.

"If you have a problem with it, Alexander, then go join some other group because this is happening. You two are getting married. I'm not going to argue with the both of you."

I can't help but look at Alexander.

He is slouching in his chair, staring at my father with his jaw clenched.

"If you have such a problem marrying me then maybe go join some other trashy group who will skin your ass alive. As if I want to marry a stuck up prick like you."

Alexander turns his head to look at me and his lips lift in a smirk. "I love pissing you off."

I roll my eyes and look at my father. "So, when is the wedding happening?"

"Engagement party is tomorrow, and the wedding is in the next few days. Thalia, you have a dress fitting before then and Alexander you have a suit fitting. I want to have this wedding happen before the time the ball comes around."

Ah yes.

The yearly mafia ball that the groups hold every year.

Every year some crazy shit happens so I wouldn't be surprised if something happened this year.

Thirty Three

I LOOK AT MYSELF IN THE MIRROR AND TRAIL MY EYES down the white sparkly dress.

Today is the day.

Aren't girls supposed to be excited about their wedding?

I feel nervous and then also bummed out because of the reason for the wedding even happening. If I want to have a wedding, I want to do it with someone I like not someone who makes my blood boil.

Even though sometimes he makes my blood boil in a good way.

But that's rare.

"You look beautiful, Thalia," my mom says and walks up to me. I stare at her from the mirror. "I am sorry."

I turn around and look at her. "It's not your fault. I can't always get what I want." I give her a small smile.

"I want you to have something," my mom says and then grabs

the back of her necklace and takes it off. "This is the necklace that my father gave me." My mom puts the necklace around my neck, and I look down at it. "I remember how terrified he was when he walked me down the aisle," my mom says with a small, sad smile.

My grandfather died of cancer a few years ago and my mom was so hurt along with my grandmother. I was very close with him and that's probably because he was always there when I needed him to be. He also taught me a lot of what I know today like combat moves.

"I miss him."

"I do too," my mom smiles at me with tears in her eyes, and she kisses my cheek. "I need to go to my seat, but I will see you out there. Your dad should be here soon."

My mom leaves the room and I look back in the mirror and trail my eyes down the dress again.

You can do this.

You are strong, you are beautiful, you are powerful.

You can do this.

I smile at myself in the mirror, and I hear the door open making me turn around and see my dad.

"You look gorgeous, *principessa*," my dad smiles. He never really smiles. He always has a ghost smile, but this is one of the rare times that he does show a genuine smile. Only time he really does smile is probably when my mom is around. I smile back at him. "You know I wish that we could have done all of this under different circumstances, right?"

I nod my head. "I know, but you gotta do what you gotta do."

"I'm sorry. I hate doing things like this, it's something my father would do. I feel like I am doing wrong."

I walk closer to my dad and hug him. "You're not doing anything wrong. You are just trying to do what's right for the Mafia and I understand."

"You are going to be a great leader, Thalia," my dad says and then he kisses my head. "Ready to go?"

I unwrap my arms from around him and nod my head. My dad takes my hand and then we walk out of the room together.

As my dad and I walk closer to the room where the wedding is being held, I start to hear music playing.

I look at my dad. "I'm nervous."

He chuckles. "Don't be. You have no reason to be nervous. You look beautiful."

I let out a small sigh before my dad pulls me out of the small hallway. As we walk down the aisle I hear the music playing and I see a lot of people.

I see people from different mafias sitting in the back of the room and then my family sitting in the front rows along with some of Alexander's family.

God I am never nervous, what the fuck?

Why am I so nervous?

It's fucking Alexander Russo, there is nothing to be nervous about.

"Take care of her," my dad says with a smile on his face to Alexander and he nods his head. My dad wraps his arms around me and hugs me. "There are multiple different groups sitting in the back so please, please make them believe this is real," he whispers in my ear.

"I will," I whisper back.

"I love you," my dad kisses my cheek and then smiles at me before walking to his seat next to my mom.

I walk up to the small stage they have set up and stand in front of Alexander.

He is wearing a black suit with a black tie. His hair looks like it got cut. He is also wearing a flashy watch on his wrist.

"You look good," Alexander says softly.

"I guess you don't look like a bird."

I am only teasing.

Alexander looks good.

But I don't want to say or admit that.

"We are gathered here today to celebrate the wedding between Thalia De Luca and Alexander Russo," the priest starts. "Marriage is a very hard thing, but it is also one of the most prized memories that couples have together."

Yea right.

"One day when you meet someone who will see the universe that was knitted into your bones, and the embers of the galaxies glow to life in your eyes. And you will finally know what love is supposed to feel like…"

The priest kept saying a few words while I just stare at Alexander, admiring all his features.

He does look good.

Why does he have to be attractive?

"Now Thalia, repeat after me," the priest says, making me focus back on him. "I, Thalia De Luca, take you, Alexander Russo, to be my lawfully wedded husband, to have and to hold, from this day forward, for better, for worse, for richer, for poorer, in sickness and in health, until death do us part."

I put on a fake smile and repeat the priest. "I, Thalia De Luca, take you, Alexander Russo, to be my lawfully wedded husband, to have and to hold from this day forward, for better, for worse, for richer, for poorer, in sickness and in health, until death do us part."

The priest turns to Alexander. "Repeat after me. I, Alexander Russo, take you, Thalia De Luca, to be my lawfully wedded wife, to have and to hold from this day forward, for better, for worse, for richer, for poorer, in sickness and in health, until death do us part."

"I, Alexander Russo, take you, Thalia De Luca, to be my lawfully wedded wife, to have and to hold from this day forward, for better, for worse, for richer, for poorer, in sickness and in health, until death do us part," Alexander says while taking my hands in his.

"You may kiss the bride." Before I can protest, Alexander walks forward and captures my lips with his.

For a moment it feels like it's just Alexander and I in the room. It is just us in a bed of sheets kissing one another, feeling passion within our bones.

It is perfect.

I almost let out a small whimper when he takes his lips off mine.

Shit.

Thalia what the fuck?

Really? In front of a whole ass audience.

"Looks like you are stuck with me, angel." Alexander smirks while looking down at me.

"Oh, joy," I mutter.

Thirty Four

Today I am going to talk to Killian. I would have talked to him a few days ago but I have been preoccupied with the wedding.

The wedding was yesterday and after the ceremony we just took pictures, and everyone went home.

Today my father is showing Alexander and me the new house. I am kind of excited to see what the house will look like because my dad designed it himself. But before going to the house I want to talk to Killian.

I leave the living room and walk upstairs to Killian's room. I knock on his door but I don't hear anything, so I just open the door. I get inside and his room is pitch black. I walk to the window and open the blinds and the window to get some fresh air in here.

"The fuck are you doing?" Killian groans and then lifts the blanket to cover his head. "Turn the fucking window off!"

I roll my eyes. "I can't turn a window off, jackass." I take the blanket off of him and he is just in a pair of sweatpants. My eyes zone in on his chest and I see a tattoo. "When the fuck did you get that?" I ask, pointing to it.

It is a tattoo of three small birds on his collarbone.

"Fuck off, Thal," he groans and then lays on his stomach. "Don't you have some stuff to move or something?"

"I'm not leaving," I deadpan.

Killian turns around and glares at me. "What the fuck do you need Thalia?"

I sigh and sit at the end of his bed. "What's going on with you? You are acting like a dick."

"Sorry, I'm an asshole," Killian chuckles.

"Seriously Killian, you are never like this. I don't know if it's your boy hormones acting out or if something happened, but you can't stay in your room forever and act like a dick to everyone."

"You don't know shit. Go argue with Alexander about his life choices instead of worrying about mine."

I don't want to leave him because I am scared about what he's thinking about. I am scared for Killian because he never acts like this, and I have lost someone because I didn't help or talk to them. I'm not trying to lose my brother.

"Ok. But I want you to know that I am here for you no matter what Killian. You can talk to me about whatever," I say, assuring him.

Killian doesn't say anything back, so I leave his room and walk downstairs.

I take my phone out of my pocket and dial my dad's number. "Hello?" my dad says once he answers the phone.

"Hey, Dad," I reply.

"Hi, *principessa,* where are you? Are you heading to the location I sent you?"

"I just got done talking to Killian, so I am on my way to the house now," I say while walking out the front door and heading to my car.

"How did that go?"

"I am worried about him. Like he is just acting weird. I also found a tattoo on his chest. Did you know about that?"

"Yeah, I did." I get inside my car and the Bluetooth connects to the car.

"What's it about?" I ask.

"A girl at school. Her name was Robin."

I furrow my eyebrows. "Robin? Why does he have a tattoo about a girl?"

"I don't know. When I asked him about it, he just shrugged me off. I have no clue what to do Thalia. I mean you were a bitch to me and your mother, but Killian is something else."

I chuckle. "Well, I turned out okay, right?"

"Yes, you did. But Killian is just going through something so I think maybe just give him some space and let him come to us, but I will try talking to him again."

"Okay. I am close so I will see you in a bit," I say and then hang up the phone.

The drive to this new house isn't far.

When I pull up to the house, I am starstruck. It looks beautiful and it is also right up on the hill with the ocean down the hill. I park my car next to my dad's dark red Bugatti which is parked next to Alexander's blacked-out Audi.

I get out of my car and look around while walking towards the entrance of the house.

"Like it?" I turn around and see my dad.

"Yes. It's nice," I say walking closer to him. "You did an awesome job, dad."

"Thanks," my dad smiles. "Alexander is inside."

Great.

We both walk inside the house and again I am starstruck by the interior of the house. It's all so beautiful.

"Dad, damn you did one hell of a job."

"Appreciate it," he chuckles. "There are five rooms upstairs and then two downstairs. The gym is out in the backyard along with a pool and grill. There is also a downstairs where you can do anything you want with that. There is more stuff, but you can explore more later."

"It's amazing dad, thank you," I smile at him.

"Stop saying thank you," my dad laughs and again it's one of my favorite things when he does that because he looks so happy.

I laugh along with him. But I stop once I see Alexander walk towards us. He is wearing a damn suit and tie.

God, why does he have to wear those?

Oh my god, Thalia, it's just a suit and tie, it's nothing.

"Alexander."

"Angel," Alexander smirks, making me roll my eyes. He chuckles lightly and looks at my dad. "So why did you call us here, Ace?"

"Well, as you two know, you will move in with each other. Obviously, you don't have to act buddie buddie, but it's what has to happen," my dad shrugs his shoulders. "Also, there is one more thing I need from you two."

I look at my dad and raise my eyebrows at him. "What is it?"

"Well, the mafia ball is coming up, so I just wanted to let you guys know."

"Who is hosting it?'

"Leo."

"Why not you?" I ask.

My dad then had a straight face. "I don't do those kinds of things."

Thirty Five

Last night was Thalia and my first night in the house.

Ace had this place designed perfectly for us. I always thought Ace was a great interior designer and I even remember my parents joking around one night saying that Ace should be a home designer instead of a mob boss.

I know Ace even designed his own house as an engagement gift for Aria.

It's funny how he is an asshole to everyone, sometimes even his kids, but to Aria?

He will do anything and everything for her.

It's crazy how obsessed he is when it comes to her.

All thoughts about Ace go out the window when I see his daughter walk inside the kitchen with only a white t-shirt on.

No pants.

Fucking tease.

"Is there any coffee?" Thalia asks as she reaches up and opens one of the cupboards.

My eyes go to her ass. She is wearing pink underwear with a lacy fabric.

I don't think twice before walking towards her and grabbing the back of her neck and pulling her up against me.

Her body heat on mine makes me want to drown into her. I want to be absorbed by Thalia so bad I don't even want to think about anything else but her.

"If you're going to act like a slut then you are going to get fucked like one. Don't test me today," I say as my lips graze her ear.

Thalia puts her hand on my thigh, and she pushes her ass into my hips. "You hard, Xander?" Thalia whispers, seductively, turning her face towards me so that her lips are only a few centimeters from mine.

"Feeling bold today, Thalia?"

"Maybe just a little." Thalia grinds her hips back into mine.

Fuck.

My grip on her tightens and I bury my face in her hair.

Vanilla.

Sweet, sweet vanilla.

"You love teasing me, don't you?"

Thalia turns around so she is facing me. My hands are still on her hips, but her arms move away from my thighs, and they rest on my shoulders.

"Let's have dinner today. Talk shit out. We might need it."

"And after?" I raise my eyebrow.

"Well, that's completely up to you and how our conversation

goes, Xander." Thalia completely let's go of me before walking out of the kitchen.

Fucking Thalia De Luca.

It's currently six o'clock at night.

I am sitting at the table, waiting for Thalia to come down for dinner. The chef made gnocchi with homemade tomato sauce.

All the food is placed on the table. I'm just waiting patiently for Thalia fucking De Luca to grace me with her presence.

I was about to say fuck it all and leave but then I feel a touch that sparks my skin and lights it with passion.

"Finally, she's here," I mutter as I watch Thalia walk around me and sit in her seat in front of me.

Ace decided to put a medium length table for Thalia and me since it's just us two living here. "Well, I had to make some sort of dramatic suspenseful moment for you, Xander," Thalia says as she flips her hair over her shoulder.

I admire her.

Thalia De Luca has this beauty in her that I've never seen in any other girl.

Her bright green eyes and dark features make her so beautiful and eye-catching that you can't look away from her. Her attitude just makes her even more alluring and captivating.

Maybe that's why I love this girl. Maybe that's why I'm so obsessed with her because she is perfect for me.

Both of us are the same but different in a weird fucked up way.

Now the hard part is fucking telling her. She'd probably run away if I told her.

"Why are we having this dinner, Thalia?"

"Because I want to talk about what's going on with us," she says before putting food on her plate from the bowls in the middle of the table. "Something changed over the last few weeks. Things have been changing between us and we need to be on the same page. We are living together so things are different now."

"Damn right."

"So, Xander, tell me why you even started to hate me in the first place because that's the one thing that I really am interested in knowing."

I smirk.

The fact that she doesn't know makes me pissed.

"Your fifth birthday and my sixth birthday. What did I give you?"

Thalia looks at me and furrows her eyebrows. She's thinking, replaying the events that happened that day.

I wouldn't be surprised if she forgot. I remember because that's the day she broke my heart.

I was a kid, sure. But I was a kid who had a massive crush on Thalia De Luca.

"A flower from the field."

"And did you keep the flower?" I raise my eyebrow at her.

"I remember putting it in my pocket, but I couldn't find it the next day," Thalia says, which makes my head spin in a different direction.

She put it in her pocket.

"I saw you drop the flower on the field before running to your dad."

Thalia's eyebrows furrowed. "I dropped it? I thought it was in my pocket. When I got home, I remember wanting to put it somewhere safe and keep it forever like I told you. I couldn't find it though." I can't help but smile at her. I hated her for a good fifteen years because of that damn flower. Thalia starts laughing and I swear to God it's the most beautiful thing in the world. "You're fucking crazy."

"Yea I know." I laugh with her, and she just shakes her head.

"I can't believe you were pissed at me for some misunderstanding, Xander. You really are petty."

I let out another small laugh and shake my head. "Why did you hate me?"

Thalia's lips lift in a small smile and blush forms on her cheeks. "I don't think I ever hated you. I think it was always just a game between us. Who could hate who the most."

"A game?" I raise my eyebrow at her and she just nods her head. "Want to play another game?"

"What kind of game, Xander?" Thalia asks, her eyes filled with desire and lust.

Oh, it's so on.

Thirty Six

Xander stands up from his seat and walks towards me.

I look up at him as he towers over me, his hands rest on my chair looking down at me with a lustful gaze that makes the spot between my legs pulse with need.

"How about whoever falls in love first loses."

My body fills with anxiety.

He is fucking crazy.

"And what does the winner get?"

"How about so many orgasms they black out?"

My lips lift in a small, challenging smile. "I'm game."

"Great. That means you're sleeping in my room."

All of a sudden Alexander grabs me and throws me over his shoulder. "All of you in the kitchen, get the fuck out. Leave everything how it is and leave. If I find you all still here I'll shoot you all in the head one by one."

"Oh my god you're unbelievable," I mutter as Alexander walks away from the dining room and towards the stairs.

"I'm the only one allowed to hear how you moan, angel." When Alexander and I get inside the room, he puts me down and locks the door before leaning against the wall. "Remember when you stripped in Russia?" Alexander raises his eyebrow at me. My cheeks heat up. "Strip for me."

"I want you to do it," I say while touching his lower stomach.

"Do it. I'm not going to ask you again."

I smirk before taking off my dress so that I'm only wearing my pink bra and lacy underwear that I was wearing this morning.

"Like what you see?" I raise my eyebrow at him as his eyes just roam up and down my body.

"Oh, fuck yea," Alexander pushes himself off the wall and strides towards me before placing his lips on mine. The way his hands feel my body and touch me in all the right places makes me want to tear off his clothes and kiss every inch of his body. We kiss until all I feel is Alexander. My back hits the bed and Alexander just leans away from me. I open my eyes and see him just admiring me. He slowly takes off his shirt while keeping his eyes on me. Alexander walks back to the bed and his arms hold himself above me on each side of my head. "You're so beautiful."

Alexander doesn't give me time to think about what he said because he captures my lips with his. I grip his face and kiss him even deeper with a sigh. While kissing, Alexander's hand trails down to my underwear. One of my hands runs down his neck and touches his strong shoulders.

"You want me?" Alexander mutters while kissing down my neck.

"Yes," I sigh. Alexander's hand cups my pussy, and he rubs the palm into my clit. My eyes close and my head twists to the side at the feeling of his hand rubbing against me. "I need you. please."

Alexander places a few kisses on my neck and then his lips graze my ear. "Beg."

I take my hand off his shoulder and run it down his torso until I feel the button of his trousers. I reach inside until I feel his pulsing cock in my hand.

"Please, Xander," I beg while rubbing his tip with the pad of my thumb

Alexander places a single kiss on my lips before muttering, "Fuck" and backing away from me. My body feels cold as Alexander gets off me.

He turns around to get, what I assume is a condom, from the drawer and my eyes catch the tattoo on his back.

A dark, black angel wing next to a pure, white one.

He got an angel wing tattoo.

My stomach fills with butterflies as I admire the work.

"When did you get those?" I ask as Alexander turns around.

"A week before the wedding," he answers, staring into my eyes deeply.

"Why?"

"Because you're my angel, Thalia. Always have been, always will be."

"I want to feel you bare."

Alexander freezes and looks at me. "Are you sure?"

"Are you clean?"

"Yea."

"Then, I'm sure."

Alexander throws the box on the floor and then walks towards me. Our mouths mold together again, and his hand trails up my neck.

His other hand takes off my bra and then reaches down to rip off my underwear. My knees bend, hugging his waist as our bodies stick together, grinding against one another.

My eyebrows furrow when I feel his cock grind against my clit and then slide down to my entrance.

Alexander reaches down and gathers my wetness before wrapping his hand around his cock.

Then I feel him slowly push inside me.

I stop kissing him and squeeze my eyes shut as I feel him pulsating inside me. Alexander keeps kissing me on my neck and chest as he thrusts himself fully inside me. "Look down." I shake my head and my head rests on the bed. "Don't make me slip out, Thalia. Look at us." I sigh before opening my eyes and looking at Alexander and my connected bodies. My legs spread wider and his hand on my thigh grips onto me tighter as he moves inside me. "God, you feel so fucking good." Alexander groans and rests his head on my shoulder as he starts going a little rougher and faster.

My nails dig into his back as I clench onto him as he moves inside me. "Xander," I whimper, feeling the need to come already. "I need-"

"Go ahead. I'm going to keep going," Alexander says, not stopping for a second.

I feel pleasure expand in my stomach and I can't help but let out a loud moan. Alexander places his lips on mine and silences my moan, kissing me, biting my lip.

"You're so fucking perfect, Thalia," he mutters while going faster and rougher inside me.

Alexander keeps hitting that same spot that drives me out of my mind. I love this feeling. I want to keep it and put it in a bottle, then only open it when Alexander isn't around.

I love how I feel with him. I love how he makes me feel.

I love everything about Alexander Russo.

I love him.

My back arches as Alexander presses one of his hands onto my lower stomach. My eyes clench shut and I can't help but grind into him.

"Xander! Stop, please! It's too much-"

"One more, angel." Alexander thrusts into me at the same time I feel his fingers touch me. Rubbing my folds and clit as I grind into him. He presses the pads of his fingers into me while still moving inside me. "One more, baby. Come on, angel." Alexander kisses my neck and leaves marks.

I come for the second time and this time Alexander follows shortly after, thrusting deep inside me.

Thirty Seven

As I put on my earrings, I hear my room door open making me look back to see who walked in.

Killian walks in and he is wearing a suit and tie. He is also wearing his diamond stud earrings and his hair is messy, but he still managed to look decent.

"Yea?" I ask.

"Can we talk?"

Killian and I haven't talked since I said Happy Birthday to him which was a few days ago. I was doing what my dad told me and that was giving him space. Killian is obviously going through something, and I want to be there for him but I obviously don't want to pressure him into telling me.

"Of course. Let me just get my shoes."

Right now, I am in the middle of getting ready for the yearly Mafia ball. My dad told Alexander and me about it a week ago when we first moved into this house and Alexander asked me to the ball the day after.

Lately, he and I have been ehhh, civil, I guess you could call it.

There have been moments where I want to kiss him and then other moments when I want to deck him in the face. Like when I was cooking breakfast in the morning yesterday, he came into the kitchen and slapped my ass. I then kicked him in the dick. Might seem harsh but he shouldn't have slapped my ass; his fault.

But most of the time I do want to kiss him and tell him I love him. I'm just scared he doesn't feel the same way.

"So, what's up? Thought you weren't talking to me?" I ask while putting my shoes on.

"I wanted to apologize for being a dick to you."

"Why were you being one in the first place?"

"I don't know," Killian shrugs as he sits down on my bed. "I was mad."

"Mad about what?" I say as I finish putting my shoes on.

"At the world. Her name was Robin," Killian states and I look up at him. "She was uh, one of my best friends." I walk over to my bed and sit down next to Killian. "But then she died, and I guess it hurt a lot," Killian says sadly. "The world makes something so beautiful and pure and then takes it away from you and destroys it."

That explains a lot.

"Tell me about her," I state.

Killian lifts his lips a little. "She was super sarcastic and always had an attitude and a comeback to everything I would say. She was always kind to people no matter who they were, she showed sympathy for people who needed it."

"Sounds like she was one hell of a girl."

"She was," Killian says sadly.

I sighed. "Killian, she is in a good place, don't worry. They are taking care of her. I'm glad you told me though."

"I thought you deserved to know because I have been acting like a dick as I said."

"It's understandable. You lost someone you cared about."

"I didn't realize how much I cared about her until she was gone."

"Did you love her?" I ask after a few seconds of staying silent.

"I don't know."

"That bird is a Robin I'm guessing?"

"Yea. I got it after she died."

"How did she die?"

"Seizure. She had type 1 diabetes and her sugar went low causing her to have one and no one was around to give her the shot thing."

"I'm so sorry, Killian. But that's life. It's a cruel motherfucker."

"I just don't understand why."

"The world takes something so close and special to us when we need it the most. It's how the world works. I am not going to tell you that it's going to be okay because I know it will hurt a lot."

Killian sighs and then stands up from the bed. "Yeah, I just wanted to tell you that."

I stand up from the bed. "I appreciate it." I smile at him.

"Mom, dad, and Alexander are downstairs. We are all just waiting on you. Do you want me to walk you down?"

"Sure," I say, giving him a small smile.

Killian takes my hand, and we walk out of my room. Once we

get to the stairs we walk down. When my heel touches the marble floor off the staircase, I see my parents and Alexander's head turn.

Jesus.

My eyes trail to Alexander's outfit. He is wearing a suit with a white blazer. His tie is also undone, and his hair is messy but he still looks attractive. My mother is wearing a long red dress that hugs her body perfectly. Her hair is straightened and pulled back. My father is wearing a suit and a red tie, matching with my mother.

"You look beautiful, baby," my mother says once I get to the last step in front of them.

"Thanks, mom, you look beautiful too," I say with a smile.

I then turn my head to Alexander. "You clean up good, Xander," I smirk.

Alexander chuckles lightly and walks closer to me.

He puts his hands on my waist and pulls me closer to him. He leans down so that his lips touch my ear. I feel shivers go down my body making me shiver and feel tingles in my stomach.

"And you look fucking divine, angel."

Thirty Eight

The ball is being held at this huge mansion that is near the beach on a huge cliff. It took almost an hour to get here but that's because of the traffic.

My parents, brother, Alexander, and I all came in the same limo. Leo and Emma are already here at the party because they are the hosts this year.

There are a lot of people here and a lot of expensive cars parked in front of the mansion. We get out of the limo along with my parents, brother, and Alexander.

"Ready?" Alexander asks as he puts his hand on my waist.

I look at him and smile. "Are you?" I ask raising my eyebrow at him.

"As long as you're by my side I will always be ready," Alexander smirks.

I roll my eyes and walk towards the entrance. Everyone is

dressed in elegant dresses and suits. Very formal. There are tables set up and then the stage in the front of the room.

I feel a hand being placed on my waist again and I know for a fact it is Alexander's because I know exactly what his touch feels like. It feels like I have thousands of butterflies in my stomach.

"If you don't get your hand off of me then I will cut it off, Xander."

"This is probably the most innocent part of your body that I have touched, angel and you should know that."

"Xander," I deadpan.

"Say it louder for everyone else to hear, angel," Alexander chuckles.

"Names?" one of the workers says.

He looks like the name announcer.

"Alexander and Thalia Russo," Alexander states.

"Alexander and Thalia Russo!" the announcer says before Alexander and I walk down the steps of the stairs to where the party is being held.

"Don't trip, beautiful," Alexander whispers in my ear as we walk down the stairs.

"Only if you don't trip me on purpose."

Alexander and I get to the last step of the staircase and we just stare at the crowd in front of us.

Usually, at these balls we eat food, meet other mafias, get awards, and then dance. I don't understand what the point of these balls is for.

Just making alliances?

"So, what do we do just walk around? Meet people?" Alexander asks.

"Well, since we are now the soon-to-be leaders then we should mingle. Get to know other mafias and perhaps help make alliances."

My dad talked to me about the role of being a leader and he said that he was trying to get other's input about the situation and see what other mafias would think about a female leader while a male is still present in the picture.

I haven't talked to Alexander about the leader position, but he has never talked about wanting to be the leader.

I think he couldn't care less.

"Well then let's go," Alexander says before he pulls me into the crowd.

Alexander and I just talk to other couples who are next in line for the position of being a leader.

There are many different ethnicities here and I even got to see my uncle, Alex, and cousin, Ariel. The last time I saw them was for the wedding, but we didn't get to talk much. I miss them though.

Jane is here though. She is with her parents right now, but I do want to catch up with her and see how she is doing.

"Hello, can I have everyone's attention please?" I hear Leo say from the microphone on the stage. I turn to face him. "Hope you are all enjoying your night, but I want to announce the winners for the awards tonight." Leo takes out a piece of paper. "For best seductress, I would like to present the award to Thalia Russo." I feel a smile come on my face.

"Congrats, angel. But I knew you would win," Alexander whispers in my ear.

I look at Alexander. "Let's just hope you get one too, Alexander." I leave him and go to the stage to get my award from Leo. "Thank you, Leo," I say before hugging him.

"Of course, Thalia. You deserve it."

Leo gives me my award and then I go back to my spot standing next to Alexander.

"Did I tell you how beautiful you look?" Alexander whispers in my ear as Leo announces the other awards.

"I think I remember you saying something like that."

"Well, just want to make sure you know how bad I want to take you into one of the rooms here and worship your entire body," Alexander whispers.

"Is this my reward from you for being the best seductress?" I raise my eyebrow at Alexander.

Alexander smirks. "Part of it."

"And I would like to announce the last winner, Alexander Russo for the best killer."

"Now I can give you an award," I whisper to Alexander.

Alexander's smirk wipes off and he just stares at me.

I see his eyes flash with something but before I can pinpoint what it is, his father calls him again ruining the moment.

Alexander walks away and goes to the stage where Leo congratulates him. Alexander smiles and I feel myself start to smile while watching him receive his award.

I don't know why but I can't help but feel that things between Alexander and I are different. It's possibly because we had mind-blowing sex the other day but still, I just feel myself thinking about him daily.

The other week, when we had sex it felt like love was being made but I don't know if it's one sided or not.

"Congratulations." I turn my head and look at Rowan.

"Thank you." I smile at him and then I see his eyes look at someone behind me making me turn my head and see Jane who is talking to a guy.

She is blushing and pushing hair behind her ear.

I look back at Rowan. "Stalker."

Rowan furrows his eyebrows at me. "You don't know anything."

"I like to think I do." I smirk. "Enjoy the rest of your night, Rowan." I pat his shoulder before walking away from him and towards Alexander who is walking down the stage.

"Congrats," I say to Alexander once he walks up to me.

"Want to congratulate me by dancing?" he asks once the music starts playing.

I put my award on the table next to me. "Sure."

Alexander put his award on the table next to mine and he grabs my waist before pulling me to where some people are already dancing.

"You know how to dance, right?" Alexander asks as we stand in front of one another.

"I'm a seductress," I deadpan. "Of course, I know how to dance. I have no choice but to know how to."

Alexander grabs my hand with his other hand that wasn't on my waist and then he starts to move side to side.

"The best fucking one yet," Alexander whispers. "Think you can show me your tactics?" He raises his eyebrows.

I chuckle and lean closer to him so that my lips touch the bottom of his ear. "I think you know most of my tactics, Xander."

Alexander tightens his grip on my waist. "Careful, angel. You don't want to start something you can't finish."

I smirk. "I think I'll take my chances."

Alexander chuckles and he is about to say something but then I hear bullets go off making everyone bend down and take cover.

Thirty Nine

Alexander pulls me to an empty hallway as more bullets start to go off.

"What the fuck?" I look out from the hallway and see everyone in the ballroom running out and grabbing their guns. I look back at Alexander and see him grabbing a gun out from his trousers. "Of course, you have a gun with you."

"Don't judge because I know where you hide your knife, Thalia," Alexander whispers to me and I feel my cheeks turn red by him once again. He trails his hand to my thigh and makes his way up until I feel his fingers touch my underwear making me jolt. "Wrong time to be wet, angel," Alexander chuckles.

I roll my eyes.

As if I don't know that.

"Fuck off." I push him away from me even though it hurts to do that, and I grab my knife from my underwear. "Who do you think is shooting the gun?"

"Party crashers who were mad about not being invited to the party," Alexander says before walking past me but then he quickly turns around and places his lips on mine.

He dips his tongue inside my mouth and deepens the kiss. I moan and grip his arms.

Alexander removes his lips from mine when he hears other gunshots go off along with people screaming.

"What was that for?" I ask while sounding out of breath.

"I need my little angel to keep me safe while I kill some people," Alexander winks before walking out of the hallway.

I let out a sigh before walking out of the hallway, towards one of the guys who had a gun in his hand, shooting at random people.

I knock the gun out of his hand and put the knife up to his neck. "Who do you work for?" I ask in a demanding tone. He tries to get out of my hold so then I trip him onto the floor and straddle him so he can't move, and I put his hands above his head while holding a knife to his neck. "Tell me or I'll slit your throat right here."

"You guys really should find more efficient ways to kill off an entire mafia," the guy chuckles. "You should have thought about Vladimir having a fucking brother."

Shit.

There's a brother.

I stab the guy in the throat before getting off him and looking around for Alexander. I see my mother and father back-to-back while shooting at people around them.

Goals.

I find Killian who is helping my mom and dad by beating

some people up with his bare hands and other people around them shooting guns.

My eyes then find Alexander who just knocked someone out.

"We have a problem," I state once I reach him.

"No fucking shit, Thalia," Alexander hisses.

I see someone walking towards us with a large knife, so I throw my knife towards his face making him fall to the floor. I see Alexander raise his gun near my head and then he shoots at whoever is behind me.

"Can we talk while just shooting people? Because focusing on just you and trying not to get killed will be hard," Alexander asks while looking around us.

I see someone running towards us two again. "Fine," I say before walking towards the guy and kicking him to the floor.

Thank fucking god I am wearing heels.

I stand above the guy and then stab my heel into his eye socket making him scream in terror.

I take my heel out of his eye socket and then I feel strong arms grab my waist. I look and see Alexander holding me behind him as he shoots someone in front of him. "What happened?"

"The Russians are alive, or Vladimir has a brother but I have no clue who."

"Where's your dad?" Alexander asks as he shoots guys who are coming towards us.

I look in front of me and see my father now beating the crap out of someone. A guy runs towards me and before he can get in front of me, I take my heel off and stab the guy in the chest with it, making him wince.

"It's nothing. Be thankful I wore these shoes instead of my

other heels," I say to the guy before punching him in the face and taking my heel out of his chest and stabbing him in the neck. "My dad is beating the shit out of a guy right now," I tell Alexander.

"Fuck," Alexander says while he continues to shoot people.

"What do we do? There are way too many people."

There are a lot of people helping us right now but still not enough.

"I need you to go look for a computer and see what you can find on the Ivanovs or if there is another heir," Alexander says.

"Okay. Please be careful," I say before walking away from him. I feel someone grab my wrist and I turn around and see a guy. His fist comes close to my face before I dodge it and deck him in the face and kick him in the balls. He falls to the floor while holding his balls. I grab his hair to make him look at me. "Who is the second heir? Who do you work for?" The guy is just wincing while shaking his head from side to side. I grip his hair tighter. "Tell me or else I will stab your eye out and leave you to bleed out wishing that I killed you," I threaten.

"Cam Ivanov."

"Cam Ivanov? What does he look like?" The guy continues shaking his head. I roll my eyes and take my heel from my other foot and stab him in the eye and I use my other heel to stab him in his hand that is holding his balls. "I told you I would do that if you didn't answer my question. Have fun with that. You will be dead by the time this is over."

"Thalia!"

I was about to walk away but I hear my name get called. I get pushed to the floor and I hear a gunshot go off. I look up and I see Alexander on the floor holding his chest.

I get up and run towards Alexander.

I sit next to him and hold his head on my lap. "Stay with me, Xander, please," I say while trying to contain the tears in my eyes. "We're going to help you. We are going to get you help, don't worry," I say reassuringly while moving the hair out of his face.

"Thalia," Alexander rasps out.

"I'm here, don't worry. I'm right here. I'm not leaving you," I say as a tear trails down my cheek.

"Cameron," Alexander rasps out and then he pushes his gun towards me.

I furrow my eyebrows at him before I look up and see what he means.

"Hello, baby." I see Cameron with a smirk on his face while walking closer to me and Alexander.

"No." I shake my head from side to side. "Don't tell me you-"

"The heir to the throne," Cameron chuckles. "You could have had a king but instead you chose a weak assassin."

I look down at Alexander and see him closing his eyes, but I lightly slap his face. "Keep your eyes open please, just keep them open for me."

"Time to get over him, Thalia," Cameron raises his gun to Alexander.

Before he can shoot him, I grab the gun from Alexander and shoot Cameron multiple times making him fall to the floor.

I look back at Alexander. "Why would you save me?" I ask as more tears fall down my cheeks.

Alexander then smirks. "Because you're the only girl I love and I'm selfish enough to not want to live in a world without you rather than you living in a world without me."

Forty

My black dress has blood all over the fabric and my hands are bloody from trying to keep the pressure on Alexander's wound.

I am sitting in the family hospital waiting room with his parents, my parents, and some of my other family members. Killian is here too but he is in surgery because he got a bullet wound in the shoulder from shielding my mother.

A lot of people had to get admitted.

My father is having his men make sure there are no Russians in the country before he starts sending people off to different parts of the world to make sure they are all for sure dead.

"Killian De Luca." I look up to see a nurse with a clipboard. I stand up along with my parents and walk to her. "Your boy will be fine. He lost a lot of blood, so he just needs to rest but he is okay. He also fractured his hands, so he needs to ice them and I have them wrapped as well."

"Can we see him?" My mother asks.

I can tell how scared she was about Killian. I was scared, still am scared because there is still Alexander who we haven't heard from.

"Of course. The doctor will be speaking with the both of you shortly. He said he has some news he would like to discuss with the both of you."

My mom and dad look at one another. They both have a knowing look in their eyes but don't say anything. I don't think anything of it and just follow them to his room.

When we walk inside his room we see him sleeping.

"Thank god," my mom says once she sees him. She walks up to Killian and sits next to him on the side of the bed. She moves some of his hair out of his face and strokes his cheek. "He's okay," my mom whispers.

My dad walks towards her and rests his arms on her shoulders, hugging her from behind.

He kisses her head. "He's okay, *amore*. We're okay," he whispers.

I bite my lip and walk towards Killian who is starting to stir in his sleep making me feel relief throughout my body.

He's okay.

"What the fuck are you guys looking all sad for?" Killian asks once he wakes up, making me laugh.

I then attack him in a hug. "I was so fucking scared dude," I chuckle, as tears threaten to spill from my eyes.

"I'm not dead so you don't have to act like you care, Thalia," Killian chuckles.

I let go of him and punch him in his good shoulder. "Dick."

Killian smiles. "The biggest."

My mom then hugs Killian and he hugs her back. "I'm so happy you're okay," she whispers. "Don't ever try to save me again."

Killian lets go of her. "I won't promise that."

"If anyone will be dying for your mom, Killian, it will be me," my dad says.

"No one will be dying for anyone," my mom says looking at my dad.

My dad chuckles and kisses my mother again.

We spend another hour in Killian's room. The doctor still hasn't come to Killian's room, so we've just been waiting on him. I'm getting anxious to know what he wanted to say.

I heard Jane got admitted to the hospital as well. Someone found her outside on the balcony, passed out. Right now, she is sleeping and they are doing exams on her. I plan on visiting her once she is awake.

Eventually we see Leo and Emma walk in with sadness across their faces.

No.

I stand up. "What happened?"

"He is in a coma from the surgery, but the doctors don't know what will happen. They said he needs a miracle and that he is fighting but they don't know what to do," Emma says.

I try not to cry. "Can I see him?" I ask and she nods her head. Before I go, I hug them both without saying anything and then I leave the room to run to Alexander's. I walk inside and I feel another tear slip from my eye. "Jesus, Xander."

His eyes are closed and he is hooked up to multiple machines. The sight looks scary.

I walk further into the room and sit on the chair next to his bed. "I can't believe I'm going to do this," I whisper. "Alexander Russo, my enemy, my old best friend, the guy I want to kiss the most but also shoot the most." I let out a sob. "Killian told me that he lost someone he cared about a lot and after she died, he realized that he loved her. He didn't tell me that but I could tell. I think that's what's happening right now. I feel like I always did but I didn't want to admit it to myself because you're right, I was a scared bitch," I chuckle lightly. "But you, Alexander Russo, are the one person to make me feel so happy and so fucking alive. I feel like I can breathe when I am around you. I feel safe and loved."

I stand up and walk closer to his bed. "I, Thalia De Luca slash Russo, love you, Alexander Russo. I know you said that you are selfish enough to have you die instead of me but I don't want you to be selfish right now. I know I told you that love isn't real but now I know what everyone is talking about when they say they are in love," I take a deep breath and a few more tears escape as I let a sob out. "I wish I a week ago when we made love."

Fuck, I never cry.

Of course, Alexander Russo is making me cry.

"You can let go. I will be okay and so will your mom and dad, I will take care of them. I know how hard it is to fight and I don't want you to anymore. I know you're probably hurting so much to fight your way back. You can let go," I say before pressing a kiss to his lips softly while trying to hold in my tears.

He doesn't kiss back which makes tears come out of my eyes. I remove my lips from his and kiss his forehead. I lean my head on his stomach and wrap my arms around him.

I let out a sob when I don't feel his arms wrap around me.

"I love you, Alexander," I say before crying into his stomach and holding him.

Forty One

SIX YEARS LATER

"Baby, we got to go!" I yell from the kitchen as I grab the flowers and my car keys.

I hear footsteps come from upstairs and I see Landon in a gray jacket with dark blue jeans on.

"Is it okay if I wear this?" Landon asks.

I smile and walk towards him and kneel so that I am at his height. "Of course, baby. You look perfect." I kiss him on his cheek and then stand up. "Now we have to go because grandpa is going to be there before us." I take Landon's hand, and he holds the flowers in his other tiny hand.

"Is uncle Killian coming too?"

"Of course, he is."

Landon and I walk out of the house, and I lock the door. We both get inside my car and he gets situated in his car seat.

I am so thankful that he isn't a baby anymore because if he was then I was probably one more breakdown away from breaking the damn thing.

"Mommy," Landon asks, making me look in the rearview mirror to look at him.

"Yes, baby?"

"I wish I could meet him."

The small smile on my face wipes away. "I know. I'm sorry."

The rest of the drive is silent and once I arrive, I park the car in the parking lot. I get out of the car and then go to the other side of the car to get Landon. I hold Landon's hand as we walk towards his father's headstone.

Once we are standing in front of it, I give the flowers to Landon, and he puts them down in front of it.

ALEXANDER RUSSO
AN AMAZING SON, A LOYAL FRIEND, AN UNFORGETTABLE HUSBAND

I found out I was pregnant a few weeks after Alexander died. At first, I didn't want to keep it and I was going to get an abortion because I didn't feel like taking care of someone when Alexander died but then I started thinking about what Alexander would want since he is the father. He would want me to keep the baby and try to move on.

After the night of the ball, I was heartbroken. I didn't eat or sleep, which was bad for the baby, but my family helped me. Thank God the Russian problem was finally solved though, at least for now it is. My father is trying to make sure everything is okay along with Killian since he is now taking the lead of the boss.

When I found out that Cameron's whole life here was just a front I was shocked. Cameron has been on this mission, trying to kill me and my family for almost my entire life, with his brother.

But when I had Landon, it felt like something beautiful entered my life and made it brighter. He looks exactly like Alexander but with some of my features. He has light brown hair and hazel eyes. He also has Alexander's ears and lips. Every time I look at him, I see a smaller version of Alexander from when we were five.

"Hi, daddy," Landon says. He likes to talk to Alexander every time we visit. "Today momma and I had eggs and bacon for breakfast. She said it was your favorite. We also drew pictures last night too. I drew one of you, momma, and I." I showed Landon some pictures of Alexander because he wanted to see what his father looked like. He said that he looked cool which made me laugh. "I miss you. I wish I could see you." Landon then kisses the headstone and I try not to let a tear slip but when it does Landon sees and he comes up to me and wraps his tiny arms around me. I let out another sob and wrap my arms around him. "It's okay, momma. You can cry."

I don't like crying in front of him. I want to be strong for him.

I'm not going to lie; this whole parent thing has been so hard. But with my dad, Killian, and Alexander's parents have been super helpful. Jane also decided to move in with me for a good year to help me out.

Things with my mom have been getting worse, slowly.

I found out she has cancer a few years ago, around the time Landon was born.

She is dying, I know she is.

But I don't want to admit it.

She is at home right now with Killian because he is waiting for the hospice to get to the house so he could come here. My dad wanted to stay with her but she forced him to come today.

"I'm sorry, Landon. I'm so sorry."

I still blame myself for Alexander taking a shot for me.

If I was paying attention, then he wouldn't have died.

My mother and father know that it's not my fault, but I blame myself every day.

"It's okay, momma. I'm here. I will always be here," he whispers in my ear. "I love you, momma."

"I love you, Landon. I always will," I say softly. I let go of him and put a fake smile on. "I think Grandpa is here." I look behind him and see my father's car coming in.

"He is?" Landon turns his head and smiles before running.

I smile while watching him before turning to Alexander's stone.

"Hi," I say while trying not to cry. "I can't believe it's been six years. I feel guilty every day." A tear slips from my eye. "Why'd you leave? Why did you have to take the bullet Alexander? You weren't supposed to save me, Xander. You were supposed to be like everyone else and just let me take it." I turn my head away as more tears start to fall. I bite my lip to hold back the tears, but it doesn't work. "Jane comes over every day to make sure I'm okay but I don't know if I ever will be. It helps that she lives close by. Landon looks just like you and every time I look at him, I feel like breaking down, but he also fills that void of you not being here," I sob. "*I lost myself in you and then I lost you.*"

I feel a hand being placed on my shoulder and all of a sudden, I don't feel alone anymore or feel like my heart turned completely black. It's like a switch in my body flipped and all that darkness and sadness washed away with one single touch only one person could make me feel.

"If only you knew how wrong you are," a familiar voice says, and I feel like I am dying from holding my breath too long. I stand up but don't turn around, still staring at Alexander's grave. "I told you before and I am going to tell you again. I am a selfish motherfucker. I would rather die than live in a world without you, rather than you living in a world without me."

I shake my head as some more tears escape my eyes. "No," I whisper.

"Turn around and look at me, angel."

I nip at my lip and turn only to see Alexander Russo staring back at me.

No.

I don't know what to say.

Was I finally going crazy?

"You can't be here."

Alexander walks closer to me, and I flinch when he puts his hands on my face. "I can prove to you how here I am," Alexander smirks and I laugh. Alexander leans down and captures my lips with his and I hold onto him as if he is going to disappear again. "You have no clue how much I fucking missed your lips. Your body, your voice, your touch, your fucking attitude," he says against my lips, and I chuckle and let out a sob.

"How are you here?" I say as tears fall down my face.

Alexander lifts my face so I can look directly at him. "If only you knew how hard I really fought, Thalia."

Forty Two

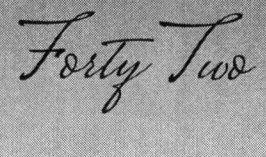

For those six years, in and out of unconsciousness all I thought about was Thalia fucking De Luca.

But then again, my mind was never not on her. Thalia De Luca corrupted my thoughts, even when I was on my deathbed, she was the only thing on my mind.

"If only you knew how much I fought for you, Thalia," I whisper while holding her in my arms.

"If only you knew how much I hate myself because of you, Xander," Thalia looks up at me and her eyes are still puffy from crying. "How?"

Good question.

Let's first start off with how I fucking got shot by that fucker, Cameron.

I fell into a deep coma for six years, I guess. At least that's what the doctors told me when I woke up.

My mother and father came once they heard the news, I was

awake. I tried leaving but they forced me to stay so that they could explain everything to me and talk about what has happened while getting some actual food in my system and the rest I needed.

I have to wait about a month for me to become fully better and back on my feet again. I wanted to see Thalia during that month. All I thought about was her while and my parents would always show me pictures of her and talk to me about Landon while I was healing.

I missed her.

"My parents decided to keep me alive instead of pulling the plug," I joke, trying to lighten the mood. "They thought that since you already poured your heart out to me on my deathbed, they didn't want to tell you so they kept it a secret from you and pulled off a fake funeral for me and fast forward to now I am alive and standing in front of you trying to keep my dick in my pants because I am a horny motherfucker right now just staring at you," I tease and Thalia chuckles before jumping in my arms and kissing me.

"I hate them," Thalia says while still kissing me. "I hate them for keeping you away from me and making me feel so vulnerable and alone."

"But you weren't alone," I state and then Thalia looks down at me.

"Did you meet him?" Thalia asks softly.

"No. I'm scared."

I am.

I am scared of meeting my son, Landon Russo.

I am scared of what he will think of me.

"Who told you about him?"

"My parents. They caught me up on everything. At first, I had no clue how to react and then I was mad at them because they kept you and him away from me."

"He thinks you're dead," Thalia states. "I have no clue what to do Alexander and-"

I cut off Thalia who is rambling. "Hey." She looks up at me. "I have no clue what to do either. I woke up like a month ago. I should still be at the hospital but instead, I'm here figuring out how the fuck I should introduce myself to my son."

Thalia gets out of my arms and she grabs my hand. "Let's go meet him then."

I take a deep breath and walk with her towards where her parents are.

For fucks sake I haven't even seen them.

I was hoping that the first person I would see would be Thalia but obviously, that's not how things worked.

As we walk closer, I only see Ace with his back turned towards me. My mind immediately goes back to what my parents told me.

Aria De Luca is supposed to die soon from cancer. My parents found out she had cancer a few days before me and Thalia's wedding. But they didn't tell Thalia until Aria fell down the stairs one night a few weeks after Thalia found out she was pregnant. Aria told her then and they cried together as Thalia held onto Aria, hoping she would never leave her arms.

Leaves crush behind me, and Ace turns his head.

His face is filled with shocked as he looks at me.

"That's not possible," Ace states, looking up and down at me. Ace walks closer to me, and I stop walking with Thalia, whose hand I am still holding. Ace trails his eyes all over my face and then he looks at Thalia who has dried tears on her face and a small smile. "I always knew you would make my daughter cry," Ace says before pulling me into a hug.

I chuckle and hug him back.

I am about to say something but then I hear the door to the bathroom a few feet away open, making me look away from Ace and look behind him.

I see a little kid who has dark blonde hair, almost brown.

He looks like a miniature me.

It is scary as fuck to see him.

"Mommy, why is everyone crying?" the boy asks while looking at Thalia.

Thalia tries to contain her tears as she walks closer to him and picks him up. "Baby. I want you to meet someone." Ace let's go of me and I walk closer to Thalia and the little boy. The little boy looks at me and I can see the confusion on his face spread. "Meet Alexander Russo. Your dad," Thalia says softly.

I don't say anything.

I stand still and study him and his expressions.

I stand so still as if he is a ticking time bomb, and he will explode.

"Dad?" The boy looks up at Thalia and raises his eyebrows. "Daddy's not here though." He looks back at me.

"Turns out, he was here all along." Thalia looks at me with a soft smile. "Alexander. Meet your son Landon Russo."

I look down at Landon and compare him and Thalia since they are side by side.

He took some of her features, but he looks more like me.

I put my hand out to Landon. "Nice to meet you, Landon."

Landon inspects my hand and looks at Thalia. Thalia nods her head and Landon puts his hand in mine.

"Nice to meet you," Landon states and I can't help but laugh.

If you told me that Thalia and I would be in love, she would be my wife, having my child, me dying then coming back to fucking life and meeting my son this way, I would have died from laughter and choked on my own spit.

Epilogue
ONE YEAR LATER

THE FEELING OF SOFT LIPS ON MY THIGHS MAKES ME stir in my sleep. My eyes open and I look to my side but don't see Alexander.

I feel a pair of hands slide up my thigh before a pair of lips kiss me in between my legs.

My eyes close and I can't help but moan softly.

"Xander. What are you doing?" I grind into his face as he continues to lick and kiss me.

"Waking up the birthday girl," I hear him say before pulling me closer to his face and dragging his tongue up and down my folds.

It's not long before I drag my fingers into his hair and press his face into me.

Alexander comes up from under the covers with a smirk on his face. His lips press onto mine and I can't help but kiss him back, despite me not brushing my teeth.

"Fucking beautiful," he mutters as he holds himself above me. "You're so perfect." Alexander smiles against the kiss.

"Interesting choice of waking me up," I say as he removes his lips from mine.

"I always love waking you like this."

"Okay what if Landon hears?" I raise my eyebrow at Alexander.

"Fuck him. He is a little shit anyways."

Yea Landon is a little shit sometimes.

For the past year he has been growing an attitude and acting like a dick. He can't help but roll his eyes at everything we tell him and then proceed to do whatever he wants. A few weeks ago, he asked me if he could get a tattoo like Alexander.

I almost knocked that fucking kid out.

God, he pisses me off sometimes.

"So, what are we doing for our day today?"

"Well, I'm thinking we stay in bed all morning, take a nice shower, and then we could go down to the beach and hangout?"

I can't help but smile at Alexander. "I'm down. What about Landon?"

"Your dad is going to watch him today."

"My dad isn't the best when it comes to kids. He is probably going to teach Landon how to throw a knife properly."

"He'll be fine." Alexander presses his lips against mine before getting up and walking towards the shower. "Hurry up and get in the shower or else my dick might fall off."

I laugh at Alexander as he walks inside the bathroom.

I get up from the bed and run towards the bathroom.

Alexander, Landon, and I live on an Island near Greece.

I'm not the Mafia *capo*, instead Killian is.

After everything that happened, I didn't want to risk losing Alexander. I want to keep Alexander in my life forever as well as the feelings he gives me. If I lost him, I wouldn't know what to do with myself.

I love him and never want to see him leave me.

I join Alexander in the shower, and he smirks at me before pulling me closer to him and tangling his hand through my hair. Our lips touch and all sorts of sparks light up in my body and send goosebumps on my skin.

Alexander grinds into me and soon I feel him slip inside me causing a moan to fall from my lips.

"I love you so much," Alexander mutters against my lips.

I squeeze him tighter in my arms, afraid he is going to leave me.

He never would though.

That feeling he gives me is kept safe in a bottle that I'll keep forever.

"I love you."

And then we make love again.

Please keep reading for a draft of Killian De Luca

*This is a preview/draft of Killian De Luca, the fourth and final book in the De Luca series. Enjoy! *

Killian De Luca

First of all, I'm going to say straight off the bat that my story doesn't have a happy ending. This story is the reality of how fucked up life is and how much I actually hate it. I hate life so much that I want to die every single day I look at myself in the mirror. I hate that I am alive and that I am here instead of the two girls I have loved so deeply and so utterly. Now I am left alone while hating the man who is Ace De Luca. The devil everyone told me about.

Killian De Luca
NINE YEARS AGO

Wearing suits has to be my least favorite thing ever. They are uncomfortable and weird fitting. My dad says that it's a way people will respect you and my mom said it made me look handsome, but I don't care.

It's uncomfortable and doesn't make me look good.

"Thalia you're such a bitch." I muttered while Thalia kept taking pictures of me.

Dad wants us all to dress nicely because we have to go to this weird party thing that my dad's work holds every year. It's always so boring because I never have anyone to talk to.

Thalia always ends up hanging out with Jane or arguing with Alexander over everything that is bullshit.

Every time we go through this bullshit party Thalia always makes fun of me and takes pictures to send them to her stupid friends.

"Thalia stop taking pictures of your brother." Mom said while looking at Thalia with an unknown expression. "And I also told you so many times to stop cussing, Killian." My mom narrowed her eyes at me.

My mom, Aria De Luca, is one of the best-known assassins in the world. She and my dad, Ace De Luca, met when my mom was trying to kill him during her mission. They both fell in love after a long and confusing story. They had my sister Thalia and then me.

Once the driver stops the car he comes around and opens the door so that my family and I can get out of the car.

My mom is wearing a long dress with long sleeves that were off the shoulder. My father was wearing a black suit with a dark red tie matching my mother's dress. My sister is wearing a black dress where it practically goes up her ass but of course, she managed to sneak past my dad and wear that.

But my dad and Thalia did fight over what she is wearing which I didn't expect anything less. They both fight over almost anything.

After a bunch of people takes photos of us, we all head inside the large building where the gala was being held.

Some people call it a ball, but it seems more like a Gala since it's much more modern than a ball.

"Please welcome Ace and Aria De Luca!" The announcer said and I swear when people looked up at us, they were about to kneel.

My family is considered royalty but not for the right reason. People are terrified of my parents and what they have done.

My father would tell me some of his most famous and well-known missions. He also told me about his best way to scare someone off and that was fire.

I swear what he tells me about fire makes me want to touch it more.

My parents and I find our seats in the giant room. The family who is hosting the gala is part of the Bulgarian Mafia. The flight that we took here was about five hours because of a delay the pilot had.

Fucking ridiculous.

"Hello everyone! So glad you could make it to the event this year! Now we hold this event every single year." The man on the stage, probably the Bulgarian Mafia leader, started talking more and my eyes move across the room, and I see a girl with bright blue eyes staring straight at me. I furrowed my eyebrows at her, and she just smiled. We hold eye contact for another few minutes with her smiling at me and with me giving her a cold glare, until the Bulgarian asshole clears us all to go on our own. "Now I hope you all enjoy your night. I will soon announce the award winners of the year but until then enjoy."

"Dad, can I go see Jane now?" Thalia asked while giving my dad the puppy dog eyes that always work.

"Go on *prinicipessa*." My dad smiles at her, and Thalia jumps out of her seat and runs off to Jane, who is a part of the American mob.

The American Mafia is very close with the Italian Mafia which is what my mom and dad represent. My mom was originally from the American Mafia but then she fell in love with my dad.

My uncle is the leader of the Americans though.

"Can I leave?" I asked my mom who was sitting next to me.

"Where are you going to go?" My mom asked while raising one eyebrow at me.

"The balcony. Is that okay?" I asked and looked at my dad.

"Yea it's fine. Go ahead but come back to check-in, alright?"

I nod my head and get out of my seat before running towards the balcony. Every time we go to this stupid event, I always wait outside for it to be over. I'd rather do that than hang out with my sister while she mostly argues with Alexander.

I know for a fact that they both like each other though. They make it so obvious

Once I stand outside, I look up at the sky and stare at all the stars.

Here in Bulgaria, the stars seem to shine brighter than they do in Italy. I've never been to Bulgaria, so I don't know much about what there is out here.

The Bulgarian Mafia just joined the families. They have been with us for over a year, and they have already successfully topped the Mexicans in the top five.

In our organization, there are the top five mobs, and those top five mafias are the mafias that have the most shipments, money, best assassins in the field, etc. My family is and always has been first place in the top five.

"Hi." I turn my head and look at a girl who was probably a couple of inches shorter than me. She is the girl who wouldn't stop staring at me from across the room. Now that she is much closer to me, I can see her bright blue eyes from up close and then her light brown hair that looks really really soft. The dress she is wearing white "which makes her look so innocent and pure. "I'm Reign." She said with that fucking smile on her face as she thrust her hand towards me to shake.

I look down at her hand and then look back at her. "Killian," I muttered but didn't shake her hand.

"So, what are you doing out here all alone Killian?" Reign asked while looking around at the scenery in front of us.

I shrugged my shoulders. "Came to take a break."

"From what?" Reign asked as she brought her eyes back to me.

"People inside."

"You don't talk very much, do you?"

"I don't like talking to people," I stated bluntly.

"Why not?" She furrows her eyebrows, confused at what I said.

"Because it's a waste of time when they don't listen."

"I can listen." She offered while her cheeks blush a little bit. "But if you don't like to talk then I can do most of the talking. My family hates that I talk too much, and I wish there were more people I could talk to because I feel like they don't ever listen to me either." Reign rambled before looking at the sky above us. "I sometimes go outside my house and sit outside to stare at the stars. I would talk for hours to myself while looking at them. Kind of weird right?" Reign snickered.

"As long as nobody catches you talking to yourself then it's not weird."

Reign looks at me and I see a smile lift on her face, and I feel a smile lift on mine too as I see her face brighten.

"Killian, I think that you and I could be really good-" Before Reign could finish, I hear someone yell her name.

"Reign! What are you doing out here?!" I see a tall man; he looks like the one who was talking on stage in front of everyone.

He looks down at me and I see his face turn into disgust. "Why are you talking to him?!" He hissed at Reign.

I clench my fist as I see Reign try to look away from the man, who I assume is her father.

"We were just playing dad." Reign mumbles.

"You aren't here for fun!" Her father hisses.

"Hey, what's going on out here?" I look to my left and see my dad walking closer to where Reign, her father, and I were standing. "You, okay?" My dad asked me once he stood by my side. I nod my head and my dad looks in front of me and he tenses immediately. "Malcolm." My dad stated and he lifts his head from Reign to look at my father.

"Ace. Is this child yours?" Malcolm asked while glaring at me.

"Yes. What's the matter?" My dad asked with authority in his tone.

"He shouldn't be anywhere near my daughter," Malcolm said while pulling Reign closer to him.

Reign's hyper, easygoing personality vanishes, and now she shies away while still looking at me. I can't help but worry if she is okay or not.

"This is the one time a year that all families are civil, and you are really going to go after two children who are playing together? Really Malcolm? Not very mature if you ask me." My dad narrows his eyes at Malcolm.

"If he comes near my daughter one more time, I will make sure to cut his head off. Don't underestimate me, Ace. You may be the devil everyone says but I am not afraid of you." Malcolm stated and I can't help but laugh. Anyone who isn't afraid of my dad is stupid because he is the one person who makes you kneel to him by just staring at you. "Got something to say, son?" Malcolm glares at me and as I open my mouth to say something, the small voice speaks up instead.

"Let's just go, dad. Mom is probably waiting for us." Reign said while trying to pull her father away from my dad and me.

But before Malcolm does leave my dad speaks up. "Careful Malcolm. Not a lot of people walk away with two feet and a pair of eyes after threatening me." My dad warns and Malcolm looks back at him.

"You have no clue what I can do De Luca. You be careful." Malcolm said before walking away while holding Reign's hand.

The last thing I see of Reign is her bright blue eyes piercing into mine.

The De Luca Series will continue with Killian De Luca as the last and final book of the De Luca Series

Release Date TBA

Follow **@_jaclinmarie_** on Instagram for more updates

Acknowledgments

Thalia De Luca was definitely such a fun book to write. When I first wrote it I was shocked with how much my writing has changed from when I first wrote Ace De Luca, and I mean this in a good way. I like how I can now write in a more mature way, if that makes sense.

I remember being really scared to publish this book because of how different it was from Ace De Luca and Aria De Luca. The cover is very different and so is the language and dialogue in the book. But I also felt super relieved when publishing this book because I couldn't wait to hear people's opinions, definitely not my families or friends because I would hate to know if they read this book by me. I would have to explain a lot to them.

Anyways, I would first like to thank my supporters. For the past few months I have had such a rocky time but with my readers they gave me such encouraging words and I wouldn't be publishing books that I wrote without them. I genuinely thank and appreciate them so so much and I still have no clue how to show my gratitude.

I would also like to thank my editor, Antonia Salazar for helping me edit this manuscript and my cover editor, Acacia Heather who created this beautiful cover that I am obsessed with. They have been so hardworking and helpful. I can't thank them enough for all their hard work.

Again thank you to everyone who has shown me support. I cannot wait to continue this amazing journey with more stories!

It would be amazing if you could leave a review! It helps when I get criticism or feedback because that makes me a better writer! I appreciate criticism a lot and it's always good to learn knew things about my writing. A positive review always helps as well.

About the Author

Jaclin Marie is currently living in sunny California, in her first year of college. She is studying Forensics Psychology and English. In her free time, she is usually writing new, mind twisting stories that have romance, drama, and thriller in them. She is known for writing her first ever story, Ace De Luca, which was originally posted on Wattpad but is now a published paperback sold on Amazon and Barnes & Nobles.

When she isn't writing or reading, she is usually going on walks with her dog, who is SharPei, drinking coffee, or going to the gym.

She first started writing in 2020 with her first novel Ace De Luca, a mafia romance with plot twists happening throughout the book.

Made in United States
Orlando, FL
18 January 2024